T0012009

#1544

Simone Kelly

URBAN Renaissance

www.urbanbooks.net

Urban Books, LLC
300 Farmingdale Road, NY-Route 109
Farmingdale, NY 11735

ISBN 13: 978-1-64556-454-6
ISBN 10: 1-64556-454-1

First Mass Market Printing March 2023
First Trade Paperback Printing March 2022
Printed in the United States of America

10 9 8 7 6 5 4 3 2 1

Distributed by Kensington Publishing Corp.
Submit Orders to:
Customer Service
400 Hahn Road
Westminster, MD 21157-4627
Phone: 1-800-733-3000
Fax: 1-800-659-2436

Also by Simone Kelly:

Jack of All Trades, Master of None?

At Second Glance

Like a Fly on the Wall

Whispers from the Past

Dedication

This book is dedicated to my brother from another, Robert Maurice Carter II, a.k.a. "my Robbie." He left us way too soon and is missed by us all. But he's doing some magical work from up there, and we all see it. Love you and miss you, Robbie!

Acknowledgments

I'm very thankful to the team that helped bring *#1544* to life. Thank you to the Urban Books family: Carl Weber, Martha Weber, Diane Taber, and Alanna Boutin. Many thanks to the best literary coach in the business, Emily Claudette Freeman.

Whoo-hoo! One of my dreams finally came true. I'm so grateful to the **Give 'n Take Film & TV Collective,** who helped me bring *#1544* to life in a short film. Thank you, Khadijah Karriem, Zariyah Perry, Bernard and Kathy Simmons of Unique Vision LLC, G. Eric Smith, Sharice Lamb, Akachi Lamb, Shaun Sinclair, Michelle Adams, Angelica Halo, D. Robertson, Kathy Patterson-Taylor, Grady Smith, Alysha Krystal, Monet and Rod Lee, Terri Page, Tosca Carroll, Maurice "Moe Betta" Bowles, Christopher Harper, and Jerrod Delaine.

My "fam" who always has my back:

Tesha Sylvester, Danielle King, Samara King, Monica Gonzalez, Delilah Garcia, Kim Lindstrom,

Lorisa Bates, Kamesha Hall, Sofiyah Jones, and the Cultural Expressions family, Valerie Crawford, Charlotte "Bunnie" Casey, and my Yahyah, who keeps me smiling.

My Beta Reader Crew: Cheryl Kendrick, Cristina Chavez, a.k.a. Latina consultant, lol, Opal Pabarue, and Ayanna Cook. Thank you for your dedication and support!

Lastly, I want to thank **YOU**, my readers! I hope you have a great time getting to know these new characters as they take you on a wild ride. I'll see you in the next novel.

Chapter 1

Ty

There was a light knock on the door. It was gentle as if they hoped no one would hear it. I froze for a moment. My hands shook slightly as I finished typing. I rose slowly from my laptop. Butterflies were fluttering wildly in my belly. I knew that once I answered it, there was no turning back. Part of me was afraid to open Pandora's box, yet the curious side of me wanted to know for sure. Now, I would be faced with a new future and a huge reminder of my past.

Last week took me by surprise. Just when things were coming together in my life, I got the phone call that I knew I would receive someday.

A young woman's cheery voice said, "Hi, I'm looking for Mr. Fifteen forty-four."

"What? Who?"

"Fifteen forty-four. Does that number mean anything to you?"

I paused, "Uh, yeah, but how did you . . .?"

She said, "Well, I would like to meet you if that's okay. I found you. I'm so happy I found you."

The light knock tapped again, this time, a little faster, bringing me back to the present. Okay, let me pull myself together. I had to stop procrastinating. I would no longer be just a number–The unknown "Good Samaritan." No longer just Mr. 1544. What was about to unfold before me I hadn't prepared for. I never thought too much about *the big day* . . . Today was *that* day.

I looked through the peephole and saw two beautiful young girls and opened the door.

"Hi, Mr. Carter?" The Latina stood there with a nervous jitter in one leg.

I looked into her eyes. My stomach squirmed. They were big and honey colored, just like mine. Her eyelashes were long, like mine. She had full lips, and her hair was long and thick but still had curls, like mine. Mine. Mine. I mean, this was some wild shit. I looked into her face as if I were looking into a mirror. It was surreal. There was no denying that she was a part of me. My heart soared. I was so delighted, I just grabbed her and hugged her tightly.

"Oh, wow." She was surprised I would be so welcoming. She hugged me back and giggled.

"I'm glad you contacted me, Journey. You really look just like my family." I stood there in awe. "My God, you grew up so beautifully. Just beautiful. Come in, please, both of you. Come in." I turned to her incredibly attractive friend. "I'm sorry, your name?"

"Oh, this is my homegirl, Natalia. She came with me for moral support. Also, in case you turned out to be a serial killer. She knows capoeira." Journey winked.

I liked her already. She had spunk.

Natalia laughed. "Nice to meet you, Mr. Carter. Yeah, I'm like her big sis, even though she bullies me around."

"Who, meeee?" Journey pointed to her chest innocently.

She followed me down the hall to the living room. "Is now still a good time to talk?"

"Yes, yes; sure, it's fine. It's not like I didn't know you were coming."

"I know, but I thought maybe you might change your mind."

"Have a seat. You're good. So, where is your mom from?" She looked mixed.

"She's Colombian but raised in Miami. You know she was really nervous about us meeting and all."

"Well, I can understand. It's a bit awkward."

"Yeah, that, and also that she lied about you," Journey said flatly.

"How so?"

"All my life, I was told you were back in Colombia with a new family. All my life. But she got very sick a year ago, and I think the guilt was weighing on her. You know—if she died or somethin' without telling me the truth."

"Oh, so sorry to hear that. Is she okay now?"

"*Okay?* She's back 120 percent. She's always in court giving motherfuckers hell." Journey covered her mouth. "Oh, sorry. She's a beast in litigation." She sarcastically cleared her throat.

I patted her leg. "It's okay. I can handle it. Wow, a lawyer, huh?"

"One day, you'll meet her."

I nodded.

Natalia chimed in. "Are you single?"

"Yes, I am. Divorced."

They glanced at each other and smiled. Oh boy, I hope they didn't think I would get with the mother. That would be a stretch. I'll have to put that idea to a halt very soon.

Journey and Natalia were both so beautiful, yet so different. Journey was cocoa brown like me. She had an urban hippy-vibe with her long, unruly hair shaved on one side. She wore a denim jacket with rolled-up sleeves showing a tattoo on her left hand and forearm. Dark eye makeup. Crystals. A big clear one around her neck, a large purple ring, and a few crystal-beaded bracelets. They were nice, but a little too much, I thought. I know crystals were for protection, but she sure was covered if that was the case. She had a strong dramatic presence. Definitely kin to me.

On the other hand, Natalia looked like the big sister. She was dressed sharply as if she just came from working at a corporate firm with a cream dress and blazer and her small Gucci clutch. Her hair was slicked back in a bun. Natalia . . . even her name had a soft, feminine presence. Her eyes made her look as if she were part Asian, but she was Black, probably from an island like most of us mutts.

Journey's eyes scanned outside the tall windows of my living room. "You have great taste. You've done so well for yourself. This apartment is soooo beautiful." She walked closer to the window. "This view is so cool. Come look at this shit." She waved over Natalia. "Penthouse living. Legit boss moves. I'm inspired."

"Ah, you can do it too. Just some hard work and focus."

"Yeah, I know. I did my research. I read your bio on your site. Google is my best friend. You graduated magna cum laude from Columbia. Started as an investment banking analyst—Goldman Sachs and worked your way up to managing director. But then the stress of corporate America got to you, and you retired at the tender age of thirty-five."

She took an exaggerated deep breath. "Theeen you went into real estate development and blew everyone out of the water with your keen eye for finding dilapidated buildings and flipping them into multimillion-dollar hipster condos. You're the shit, Ty. I mean, really."

I laughed. She was definitely a chip off the old block, doing her research. "Come on, Journey, you can pull it off. You can do whatever you want to do." I was blushing now. "You got good genes," I smirked. I really liked the idea of being a father now.

She laughed. "Oh, you funny toooo? I guess I get that from you. My mom is so serious sometimes."

"Oh really? That's interesting." She's probably one of those busy women that never took the time to settle down because they were so focused on their career. Those, I-don't-need-a-man-for-shit kind of chicks. I'll have to school Journey not to be one of those since she'll end up alone. I'm glad I could help her out with my "donation."

"Oh, just so you know, your great-grandfather is here. He's been battling dementia for the last few years, so he can't talk much, but I'll bring him out. Have a seat."

"What? I have a *great*-grandfather?"

I went and got Papa from his room. We walked over into the living room and said hello. He didn't respond until I put the TV on and a commercial played. Then he tapped his hand to the beat of the jingle, staring at the 72-inch screen as if no one were around.

Journey whispered, "Is he always like this?"

"Pretty much. He rarely speaks, and when he does, it's mostly in Spanish."

" Oh wow, so where do your parents live, my . . . my grandparents?"

"Well, that's the thing," I sighed. "We lost them both in a car accident many years ago, right on Cheshire Bridge Road. Drunk drivers, we think. It was a hit and run."

"Oh no. That's soooo sad."

I patted Papa's knee lightly. "Yeah, it's not easy." I pointed to the family photo on the wall when I was in grad school. "I'm the only one left to take care of him. My grandma, Mercedes, was his wife. She died a few years before."

Journey leaned in. "How did you deal with that, you know, being there?"

My jaws clenched, and a chill went down my back. "Being there?"

"Yeah, at the crash."

"Wow, I don't remember it, but . . . how did . . . How did you know I was there?"

She shrugged. "Oh, I'm just weird like that. I just felt your pain."

Natalia chimed in, "It's her thing, Mr. Carter. She knows everything. It's wild."

"I haven't thought about it in years, but you're right. I *was* there. I don't really like to talk about it." The guilt of me being the only survivor still haunted me.

"Oh, I understand. No worries." Journey patted my hand.

Natalia seemed impressed and asked, "You do it all by yourself? Taking care of him?"

"Oh no, no. I have a nurse that stays a few nights a week, and she's here during the days when I'm at work. He has ample company. He's quiet, but he's a handful. No way could I do this by myself." I walked over to my office door. "Come on over here, and I can show you some photos of the fam."

Natalia said, "Hey, I'll hang out in here with your great-grandad and keep him company while you two get to know each other."

"He'd like that. He won't be much company, but he does like to look." I pointed at him. "Papa, behave, okay? Don't get fresh." I winked at Natalia.

Papa grunted as if to say shut up. I understood him, even though he rarely spoke. We had a bond, and I didn't need to hear words. I felt him. I just "feel" people. Sometimes I can just hear what they're thinking. It's a wild little trick I play with myself, and it works.

Natalia's voice was so soft and sultry. "Can I change the channel, though? It's the news. Kinda depressing." She tilted her head and smiled.

I quickly scanned her body. Nice legs too. "Sure, go ahead. But just a hint. He loves any of those court shows. *Divorce Court* makes him laugh. It's like his whole face lights up."

"Wow, that's funny," Journey said.

"Okay, I'll find a juicy court show just for Papa."

Papa surprised us all when he tapped his feet and mumbled, "Gracias."

Natalia raised her brows at me.

"I think he likes yoooou." I laughed and walked into my office with Journey.

"He seems so sweet."

"He can be a grouch too, especially when he's in pain, but he's gotten better since we've had his nurse, Jocelyn. He used to be in a wheelchair, but he's walking again due to her physical therapy. Slow, but walking nonetheless, with his cane. She's great company for him. She speaks Spanish and cooks all his favorite meals."

"That is awesome. What was he like before . . . I mean . . . before . . ."

"No, it's okay. He was actually a lot of fun. He was a very charming man who would talk about everything from politics, technology, to astrology. He was an intellectual who loved a good debate. He loved talking about Cuba and his love/hate relationship with the island. He especially loved to stress that he was Afro-Cuban. He was so proud that many of his people were beginning to embrace their Black roots since, in his time, he was discriminated against so much for being a brown-skinned Cuban. He was very proud to be Black, and he ingrained that in me as well."

"That's amazing. I wish I had that growing up. It must have been awesome growing up and hearing his stories."

"Well, many of them I heard a little later from my mom and aunts since it was more like family gossip. His real name is Pedro Garcia, but his nick-name I heard all my life was Papi Ching-Ching. I used to call him Papa Ching-Ching until I became a teen."

"Oh, that's so cute. I love that name. Where did Ching-Ching come from?"

"He had a lot of money, apparently. He was an engineer by trade, but at night, he was a musician. The rumor was he had ties to the American mob in the fifties. You know, names like Lucky Luciano?"

"Yeah, I've heard that name."

"Well, that was one of Papa's boys. They hired your great-grandmother Mercedes to be the lead singer at the Hotel Nacional. The hotel is consid-ered a national monument to this day. She got paid well, from what I hear. Papa was well connected with them. He started as a high-stakes gambler who was very lucky most of the time. It was to the point they used to call him a *Brujo* since he won so much."

"Whaaaat! He was casting spells?"

"Not at all. He had a way of reading people, and they would keep him around to watch the other gamblers and catch cheaters." I tapped my temple.

"Get out. That is *so* cool. It's in the genes."

"Yes, but the family didn't talk much about his shady dealings with the Mafia. I just know he was lucky not to get killed or put in jail. They would have called him a 'trader.' That was one of the reasons they wanted to leave when Castro took over. His wealth that he accumulated from gambling was taken."

"Wow, so much history lies within him. He looks so sweet and innocent. You would never know."

"Nope. Now, he just watches the news, courtroom TV, telenovelas, game shows, or just listens to audiobooks. It's sad to see his eyes drift off into space. I wonder what he's thinking most of the time. But he has his alert moments now and then, especially when music is on. Okay, let me not depress you. Let's look at some pictures."

"Trust me; I love every minute of this. It's not depressing me at all."

I had a stack of photo albums; some mine and others were Papa's. I knew they would give her some insight into the family tree. I was excited to show her them. She sat on the big leather love seat and looked up at all my diplomas and awards in awe.

"Daaaamn, you went to school—a lot."

"Well, yes. My parents were tremendously big on getting a good education, and it was worth it. Now, I can work for myself. Papa was an engineer for the government and a musician in Cuba. And Papi—your grandfather—was a surgeon in Cuba and also a musician. Do you play anything? I play the piano."

"I see. I saw that big grand piano in the living room. I don't play anything, but I always wanted to learn guitar."

"One day, I'll play for you."

"I'd love that. My family is so smart and talented! So, was college worth it? Student loans are a joke. I think it's the government's way of keeping us in debt forever. It's a damn scam. Almost seventy percent of people who go to college never get a job in their field."

"Okaaaay, I see you've done your research. So, what are you saying? You don't want to go to college?"

"I did a year and a half, but some personal stuff happened, so I needed a break. Now, I'm on the fence. I figure if I can't pay cash for it, it's not worth it. For the things I have planned, I don't know how much college I'll need. I just need common sense and connections."

"Oh, is that right?"

She was a confident one at such a young age. That's me again.

"Just some stuff I'm brewing up." Journey flipped through some pictures. "I'll tell you when the time comes. I want to have it all together." She turned to me and held up the album. "She is soooo pretty. Who's this?"

"That's your great-grandmother in Cuba."

"She was hot stuff. What was this, like the fifties?"

"Yes, her name was Mercedes, the singer I told you about earlier at that popular spot for the mob. She had some amazing stories. Papa snatched her up, and they were married for fifty-four years."

"Holy shit. Now, that's a commitment."

"Tell me about it," I laughed. "A bit much for me."

"So, how long have you been divorced?"

"It's been several years."

"Oh, I'm so sorry to hear that." She flipped pages.

This was so surreal. I just stared at her. She was my flesh and blood. Journey removed her jacket and had on a tank top and revealed her entire left arm was tattooed.

"Nice tat. What is that? Feathers?"

She pointed to it. Her fingers were long and had the same shape as mine. I mean, down to the nail bed. Journey said, "A peacock. It represents beauty, royalty, spirituality, and protection. I needed it to remind me of who I was. She's my protection."

"Like your spirit animal?"

"Yes. Exactly. Let me find out you are into this stuff."

"I know a little something." I popped my collar.

"Well, my mom lost her shit when I got it, though."

"Did you ask for her permission?"

Journey blew out air and rolled her eyes. "Permission? I was nineteen when I did this. I paid for it. It's my body," she shrugged.

I jerked back.

She caught herself. "I mean, I mentioned to her before I did it, but she didn't realize it would be a whole sleeve."

I could see she could be a little bit of a brat. Her mom spoiled her rotten, I'm sure. She's lucky I didn't raise her. That shit would not be up her arm. That would not fly in my house.

She leaned in and asked, "Did your parents or anyone know what *you* did?"

I tilted my head, unsure of what she meant.

She made a jerking-off motion with her hand in the air and squinted her eyes tight.

I started laughing. "Reeeeally, Journey? Reeeeally? You're a comedian, huh?"

"I'm sorry. That's how it works, though, right? Don't you put it in a cup, and they send you off to the freezer, and then they made me. Voilà!" She laughed as she fluffed up her long hair in the full-length wall mirror.

"So, are you asking if I told anyone that I was a donor? Definitely not at first. But I did tell them years later."

"Wow." She lowered her voice. "You probably got like a hundred babies out there. That doesn't freak you out? Am I the first to contact you?"

"Actually, yes. But it doesn't really freak me out. It's actually kinda exciting. I'm happy I was able to help families conceive. I highly doubt it's a hundred. They have a limit," I laughed.

"That would be one helluva child support payment."

"Tell me about it. I have enough expenses."

"Well, thank you for being a donor, Tyler. What would you like me to call you? Donor Dad? DD?"

"Ty is fine. I know 'Dad' might be a bit strange for . . . well–us both. Maybe once we get to know each other–I don't know. Were you raised by a dad or ah . . . another mom?" I awkwardly scratched my head.

"No, no, my mom is straight. No other dad. She never married. She poured everything into me and her work. It's pretty sad, actually. I like Ty. I'll stick with Ty for now." She reached in her back pocket for her cell. "Can I take a photo of some pictures on my phone to show my mom?"

"Sure, go ahead. I can make you some duplicates in the future so that you can frame them."

She was as excited as I was. She started to snap photos from the album. My mouth got dry, and I stood up to head to the kitchen.

Journey never looked up at me but said, "Just some water is fine."

I looked at her in awe. "But I didn't say anything. I was about to ask you if you wanted something to drink." I tilted my head and looked at her. She had her head deep in the albums.

"Oh, that's funny. We're connected, Pops." She laughed it off.

I poked my head into the living room. "Is everything okay out there, Natalia? You thirsty?"

"No, I'm good. It's been a little over an hour, and I really don't want to be the party pooper, but I have to get back to work. My night job."

Journey chuckled. "What—Uuuuber time?"

Her voice weakened as she mumbled, "Yeah, Uber Eats."

"Seriously? You look like you work in law."

"I work a corporate job in the day and Uber Eats at night. I'm trying to save my money for some investment properties."

"She makes bank doing Uber too. She's trying to get me to do it, but I don't want to be delivering no food to some creep in a Motel 6. I just teach private classes to build up my coins."

"I tell you one story—*one* story—and you sum up all of my deliveries to creepy men in motels," Natalia scoffed.

"I know, right?" Journey laughed. "But, Ty, oh my God. This is perfect. You know, since you do real estate, maybe you can help her. That's her passion. She's obsessed with that *Flip This House* show, *Property Brothers*, all that crap. She's always reading books on it. Are you in need of help in your office?" Journey raised her eyebrows. Her smile was convincing. It was like I heard her in my head saying, "*Say yes, say yes.*"

Natalia said, "I don't have my license yet, but I'm studying for the exam."

Her eyes were endearing, almost innocent. Her dress hugged her hips and butt just right. I saw myself peeling her out of it. "How old are you? I mean . . . um, have you graduated yet or are you still in school?"

"Oh noooo. I'm thirty-two . . . *Not* Journey's age."

"Humph. Okay, okay." I snickered. She's old enough. Twenty-five was my cutoff of how young I'd go. How perfect would that be? I can hire her to answer my phones, book appointments, or something. Maybe a personal assistant to help with Papa's endless doctors' appointments.

"Okay, Natalia." I reached in my pocket. "Send me your résumé, and we can meet up soon and see if there's any synergy." Our hands touched slightly during the business card exchange. I felt a jolt go through me, but I couldn't react. She smiled softly as if she felt it too.

She made strong eye contact, and her voice was smooth. "Great. That sounds good, and worst case, I would love to shadow you for a couple of days to see what it's like." I liked her enthusiasm.

Journey chimed in, "Hell yeah, better than any college class. I'm all for on-the-job training."

My eyes said, "Call me." My mouth said, "Let's talk soon."

Natalia blushed as if she knew, but I had to chill out. My daughter was watching. I can't believe I finally met her. My daughter—Well, one of them anyway.

Journey and Natalia left with big smiles. I was glad she decided on calling me, Ty. Dad or Pops, nope—too soon. I wasn't ready for the weight of that title. One hundred babies out there? That shit is wild even to imagine. I never even thought about it in a while, but I know I have at least seven children from the last report the sperm bank sent me.

Chapter 2

Journey

I fell back on my fluffy pillows looking at my texts from Kendu today. He was so flirty and fun. Ever since I gave him some, he's been on my phone telling me he thinks about me all day. He's good for my ego.

Kendu: Let's do Yoga together–naked.
Journey: Get up off my phone, boy. LOL.
Kendu: You're right; we'd never get to the Yoga part.
Journey: Exactly.
Kendu: Sweet dreams, beautiful. I'll call you tomorrow.
Journey: Okay. Good night, handsome.

I then checked out my other texts from my VIP clients, Philip and Mr. Candella. They were both trying to book me for my private Yoga sessions that have been in high demand lately. Even though I had one more spot open, I would rather give it to Philip than Mr. Candella. That man was so full of himself. He doesn't take instruction well, and the worst part is he only lets me address him as Mr. Candella. Give me a freakin' break! But he's an owner of a local bank, so I'll keep him on my good side in case I need a loan one day. However, he can wait until next week: supply and demand. Economics 101 taught me that.

I have to admit that I'm an amazing actress since most people wouldn't even know how much I can't stand them. I can plaster a smile on my face in Yoga even if I'm exhausted and don't want to be there. I can squeeze out a grin or giggle for bosses, associates, even my mom. I can fool them all. Many would never know that I have suffered from depression. I have dealt with loneliness, rejection, and just not fitting in. But let's just say I've learned the art of not giving a fuck. Yeah, I read that book too. So, instead of complaining, I have learned to deal with life as it comes.

From the outside looking in, you might think I'm ungrateful, a spoiled brat even. I can see why. I can't say I lived a deprived life or anything close. My mother showed me love the only way she knew how—with things. Clothes, vacations, jewelry, etc., but very rarely ever with her time. Her work as an attorney *always* came first. I think her disconnection from reality is what drove me to want to go deeper with self-reflection. To get to know *me, my* purpose, and really understand more about who I was. Not to be as materialistic as she was. I live to embrace experiences versus having the latest Gucci bag or Benz to show off. That's why I was drawn to meditation and Yoga to get connected and go deeper than the shallow shit I saw around me.

The pain of never fitting in started early on. I did everything in my power to stand out and get attention since I was an only child, from dressing in mismatched socks, putting strange colors in my hair, ripping up my jeans, and cutting my tees. I hated looking like the straitlaced preppy students in my private school. Instead, I reveled in my uniqueness. It's the only part of my identity I have 100 percent control of. Leave it up to my mother, and I'd be wearing stylish Versace dress pants and Gucci loafers or freshly pressed skirts and blouses all day. She can keep those monkey suits. I'd rather rock my relaxed Yoga gear, some jogging pants, flip-flops, or some sneakers. I'm all about *my comfort* and not trying to impress others. As long as I look and feel good, that's all that matters to me.

One may look at me and think my tattoos and piercings make me into some hipster in a Starbucks coffee shop. Okay—Okaaaay. So, I do teach Yoga, drive a Benz, indulge in green tea, smoothies, and

Chai Lattes, but I am much more than people assume. I don't mind being underestimated either since it keeps me under the radar. No one knows who I truly am.

Truth be told, I was at the top of my class in high school. I still got straight As at SCAD University in all my interior design and architecture courses. But honestly, school bores me. I could be finishing college, but I decided to take a break, at least that's what I told my mom. I don't really need college anyhow. I'm particularly good at sales, or let's just say I've mastered the art of persuasion. I'm currently building up my lifestyle brand, and even though I work at three Yoga studios right now, that is not my forever plan. I could easily run my own Yoga studio, but my dream is bigger than that.

What I want to do is open a lifestyle center within the next two to three years. It's gonna be sort of like a community and wellness center in one. There is nothing like it right now. I have some wealthy clients and friends who suggested that I do it. I have even drawn detailed sketches of it. I made a vision board for it in my room. I'll be working on the complete layout as soon as I get my location. I can see it. It will be a center for everyone, but I'll have dedicated programs funded with grants and private donors to help the homeless. It's going to be the talk of the town. It's going to help *thousands* of people. Every day on my way to class, I would see so many tents and makeshift shelters under the highways and bridges. I want to have programs to help those people rebuild their lives, help them find jobs and housing, and provide mental health and wellness programs for them.

In my research online, I found out that over 3,000 homeless people live in Atlanta. They are the forgotten people that I want to help. So many ended up homeless due to job loss, mental illness, abusive relationships, and much more.

I just need more time to figure out how to get at least 100K to start it. When I looked into how much it would cost to start it, I was told at least 50K, but I want more as a cushion. I know my mom might chip in a little. I got my side hustles going too to stack my coins. I know Ty can help with advice on real estate locations and much more once he truly sees my vision. It's going to take a little bit of convincing, but I know I can do it.

I'm sure I can even get some important politicians and community leaders there for the ribbon cutting. That would be soooo bomb. My mom is friends with the mayor, so I know it can happen. I'll be on all the radio shows and morning shows announcing it. It's going to be the talk of the town for Atlanta. A 20-something opening a center to help the less fortunate and empower all. I gotta get ready to see my name in the press. Yes, my dream *will* come true. I see it.

Natalia and my mother thought I might be reaching too big, but they don't know the whole story of why I'm so passionate about opening it. When I started college and was also in my Yoga training program, I would spend long hours at Starbucks working just for a change of scenery. I used to see this lady almost every day named Janet. I knew her name because, well, everyone knew her. I would stay late until they closed, and the manager, Santiago, was so kind to her. He would give her the leftover food that didn't sell that day since they had to throw it out anyhow.

Janet was very cordial and well liked. I would feel sorry for her, though. She had a beautiful face with deep chocolate skin, and I could tell she was probably gorgeous twenty years ago. She was a little heavyset, and although homeless, she never looked dirty or smelled bad. Janet did look as if she carried the weight of the world on her shoulders with her sagging posture and a vacant stare. If she had a little makeover, I'm sure she would be a pretty lady in her 50s. Unfortunately, the streets just seemed to suck the life out of her eyes. She wore layers of clothes that I assume were all she had since it wasn't that cold. One day I saw her come in earlier than usual. She parked her bike out front. It was adorned with a huge basket and several plastic bags hanging from it.

She came in, and one of the baristas waved at her. She smiled, grunted, then started mumbling as if speaking in secret to someone. Light jazz music played, and the blenders whirled in the background. She stared at a photo of coffee beans on the wall as she sat at a table. I stopped studying my Yoga asanas on my laptop and sipped my green tea. I said in my mind, *Who the hell is she talking to?*

She turned to me. "What? You don't see him?"

I was shocked that she answered me. I almost spit out my tea. I nervously responded, "See who?"

Her voice was raspy and aggressive. "You asked who I was talking to."

I felt a heavy feeling in my stomach. I could not believe she heard me. I panicked.

Janet's eyes widened as she stood up. "Earl. My brother Earl. He right there. You can't see his big-ass head?" She laughed and pointed in front of her where the painting on the wall hung.

I saw nothing, but somehow, I believed her. If she could *hear* my thoughts, maybe she could see the unseen spiritual world too. "I'm . . . I'm sorry." I shook my head. "I don't see Earl." Now, I was curious. "What is he saying to you?"

She slammed her hand on the table. "Finally, someone who cares." She sighed and sat back down.

I decided to give it a shot and see if I was truly imagining this. So I took a deep breath, and I said in my mind, *Can you hear me?*

"Of course, I can hear you. You sitting right next to me. I'm homeless, not deaf," she snapped. She started fumbling with one of the newspapers on the table the last customer left as if she were going to start reading it. "What's your name? I like your curly hair. I used to have nice hair back in the day." Her hair was now covered in a dark knit skully.

I didn't say a word with my mouth. *It's Journey, and thank you.* She smiled at me. Wow, was this really happening? I was amazed. All this time, I never knew I had this power. Another customer waiting in line looked back at her "talking to herself," and just shook her head.

"My name is Journey," I said again, just to be sure.

"Girl, I heard you the first time. That's a pretty name for such a pretty girl. Sorry, Earl keep running his damn mouth and talking over you." She leaned in toward me and whispered, "People think I'm crazy and wanna lock me in a padded room." Then she pointed to the air. "I'm not going back, Earl. I promise you. I'm not letting them people drug me up again," she shouted to the empty space in front of her. Then her voice softened. "You got it too. You a seer. You might not see spirits yet like me, but you sure can hear thoughts." She pointed to her temple and nodded.

I am shocked you can hear me. This is wild.

Her eyes widened as she looked at me. *Just be happy you don't get treated like me. Don't tell nobody 'cause they will put you in an institution. You don't want that. No, ma'am, you don't want that at all.* Her eyes started to well up with tears, and she bit her bottom lip as if recalling a bad memory. *Tell no one.*

That night, I bought her a sandwich and some coffee, and we became fast friends. I was in awe of her skills and so happy to uncover mine. Janet was like my practice buddy. She made me realize why I was so guarded all these years. I was an empath and had the gift of telepathy. I would see her at least three times a week and "talk" to her.

I made sure to be there the following day a few hours before closing time. She spotted me when I walked in. Janet greeted me with a wide smile. "Heeeey, pretty girl." She sat down at the table across from me.

"Hey, Janet."

I said in my mind, hoping yesterday wasn't just a fluke, *Can you teach me how to get better? I want to practice with you.*

Janet opened up a book and flipped to a dog-eared page as if she were reading it and said back to me, *I never taught anyone before. It doesn't work on everyone either. Shit, if it did, I would be at the W Hotel every night, rent free, not sleeping in the park.*

"Now that *is* funny. But now, the more I think about it, I have been doing it for a while but just never really understood it."

She spoke out softly and put her book down. "Nope, they gotta be open. You can't speak to 'everyone.' And some real good psychics, well, they know how to block you from getting in." She tapped her temple, then scooted her chair closer to me and said low, "Tell Santiago to make me Venti Hot Chocolate and bring us two lemon loaves."

I shook my head. "Are you serious? You think that will work? Hold up. Is this how you are getting free shit all the time?"

Janet put her finger over her lips and giggled so innocently. *Not really, I did it in the beginning, but now he just does it on his own.* She gave me scolding eyes and tapped her temple to say, talk in your head. She looked behind us to make sure no one was listening.

Okay, I will ask Santiago.

I looked over at him. He was on his knees restocking sandwiches, salads, and water. He was a fun and upbeat Peruvian guy in his early 30s. He was having a spirited chat with one of his baristas when I interrupted him and said in his mind, *Santiago, will you be a sweetheart and bring Janet and me two lemon loaves?*

Janet pretended to be reading her book. I was pretending to be typing. We made eye contact and smiled as Santiago got up quickly and went behind the counter. I added, *Oh, and Janet would like a Venti Hot Chocolate.*

I whispered, "Oh my God, I think he heard me."

"Yes, he did. It's usually people that are not guarded that are easier to 'break in.'"

"Break in? Wow, when you put it that way, I like that."

"Yeah, but don't abuse it. It can backfire. Give you bad headaches, even nosebleeds sometimes. It won't work for long if you're a greedy person. I believe in Karma, baby girl. I had enough bad luck in my youth for abusing it. Don't need it no mo'," she snickered.

I leaned in and thought, *So, let me understand this. People who can break in, those are people who are what . . . just gullible or open-minded?*

They are people who live with their guards down. They usually just trust you, naturally loving folk, like you, Journey.

She said softly, "That's why I know you good people. But like I said, we shouldn't do it too much since you still learning. You gonna get headaches."

"Oh well, that's good to know, and, Janet, you are more than good people. You are changing my life right now."

Just then, I heard fast, small steps coming behind me, and Janet motioned with her chin for me to turn around. Behind me was a smiling Santiago, holding two lemon loaves and hot cocoa for Janet.

I laughed so hard. "Wow, Santiago, don't be rushing up behind me like that."

"What, you don't want it?" He put the cake down for me and handed Janet hers.

"No, no, this is so kind of you. You scared me. What made you bring—"

"I don't know," he shrugged. "Maybe I just like you two. I see you are besties now." He winked and sashayed away.

"I love yoooou." Janet blew a kiss in his direction.

"Enjoy, ladies." He went back to stocking the fridge. Janet sipped her hot chocolate and mumbled, "You got the gift, guuuurl."

I said, "No fucking way is this really happening." My eyes widened as I looked back at him. "This is nuts." I took a nice bite out of the sweet cake. We both had huge smiles of satisfaction across our faces in between our nibbles.

"Soooo, Janet—I meant to ask you, what happened to your brother, Earl? Why is he always around you?"

"Oh, Earl. His goofy ass was going through a midlife crisis and wanna go buy a motorcycle at 47 and got himself killed on I-85. They said he was speeding. Went right into a rail. He was my only sibling and my best friend. Now, he feels guilty for leaving me and been trying to get me off the streets to live with his family. But I ain't doing it. They tried to put me in a mental institution before. He been gone five long years, but it feels like he never left. I see him clear as day, as if he right there." She pointed to the wall. "I see him in my dreams. I always saw spirits and heard people's thoughts, but I had more control over it when I was younger. It got worse after I lost my job. I got laid off from my job at the Publix warehouse. Then the voices in my head got worse."

"Oh, I'm so sorry to hear this, Janet."

"Yeah, I started drinking more, like heavy dark liquor to numb the break ins. But it was like so many voices at once. It was overwhelming. Drinking helped, but it ain't do nothing but send me more downhill."

"Shit. Did you finally stop?"

"Oh yeah, I haven't touched the stuff in like a year. Stopped cold turkey. Earl made me check into a rehab. It was okay at first, but then they was diagnosing me wrong, calling me a schizo and shit."

"Oh noooo, that's terrible."

"The labels was one thing, but the drugs. Journeeeey, guuuurl. The shit they give you for anxiety and for being schizophrenic make you just wanna curl up and die. Makes you sluggish. I felt like a zombie for real. But the voices stopped. I didn't want them to stop, just slow down. Earl was all I had left, and I didn't even hear or see him no more. I cried, prayed, and begged God to let him come back."

I patted her hand and smiled. "Well, now, he won't leave you alone."

"Okaaaay. Be careful what you wish for."

I looked at her many bags on the floor. "How is it living on the streets? Aren't you scared?"

"Oh no, child. I used to be, but I know where to stay. We aren't bad people, for the most part, you know? Many of us help one another out. We know the little towns to stay at. Do you know, like right off of eighty-five? Have you seen all of them tents?"

"Yes, I always wondered how that community worked."

"Oh, it works. I used to live there. It's called The Hill. But it's really a hill of trash. About sixty to almost one hundred people live there now with about 500 rats and a million and one bugs," she laughed. "I couldn't take it. Got too nasty for me."

"Oh, hell noooo. I don't do rats or bugs."

"They will eat all your snacks and gnaw on your clothes." She pressed her lips together in disgust. "But we did have running water, a shower, and even a barber."

"Get out. That's amazing when people pull together."

"It works for some people, but I couldn't do it for more than two weeks. I go to visit and barter stuff when I need to, though."

"You wouldn't try a shelter?"

"Nah, they never have room, and you got to sleep with one eye open. It's like being in jail. I got my hiding spots in the park for now that are pretty safe. So don't worry about me, pretty girl."

A beautiful, tall, blond lady walked in. She wore a dark suit and stilettos. Corporate classy was her style. Janet tapped her temple.

Okay, we gonna make her think she got a spider in her hair.

Oh, Janet, that's so mean, I snickered.

Janet's eyes tightened as she folded her arms. *Oh noooo, the hell it ain't. She's a snobby, stuck-up bitch. She always clutches her purse or moves it to the other side of her table whenever I walk by her. She doesn't even look me in my face, like I'm beneath her.*

Say no more. So, how do I do it . . . just picture a spider?

No, you tell her. There is something in your hair. Scream it if you have to. Janet was smiling so hard now. She loved revenge like me.

I took a deep breath and just focused on her bun. Then I pictured a spider hatching 100 eggs, and I yelled into her mind.

There's a spider in your hair. She's laying eggs. Get them out. Get them out.

Janet looked at me instantly. Her brows furrowed, and my mouth opened when the lady started to scratch the back of her head under her bun. It started lightly at first. Then after she paid for her coffee, she told the barista she would be right back. She did a light jog to the bathroom and came out five minutes later with her hair flowing down to her shoulders.

My gaze ping-ponged between Janet and the woman. I got nervous and then pretended to be typing and looked over at Janet.

"Oh shit. I did it."

She laughed a deep laugh. *She was up in there, checking each strand. She probably thought her ass had lice.*

I bit my bottom lip. *Oh, I feel horrible.*

"Don't. People like her need a little wake-up call now and then, but let me stop being a bad influence. We can't do that too much. Karma."

"I feel you. It's probably good I didn't learn this as a teenager. I had a temper on me then."

Janet laughed. "Yeah, it will come back to bite you. That's why I stay clear of people. I keep to myself."

"But don't you ever get lonely, Janet?"

"Nope, I know a lot of people. People look out for me, so I'm good. And hey, I got you as a friend now too." She smiled and sipped her hot chocolate.

One thing is for sure. If you took away the layers of clothes and her bike with all the plastic bags hanging on it, you would never know Janet was homeless. After a couple of weeks of getting to know her, she began to open up more. She told me she showered a few times a week at the shelters or took bird baths in gas stations or supermarket bathrooms. That broke my heart, and I figured out a way to sneak her into one of my Yoga studios at night to get a hot shower. I felt it was time to find her a place to stay, even if she claimed she was okay. Her pride was something else. I mean, who would want to sleep on park benches every night? I spoke to one of my students who works in a wellness facility to help women get back on their feet, and they found a room for Janet—for free. It took a little convincing, but once she did her own research and learned it was not a psychiatric hospital, she was all in.

We stood in the parking lot with her bags. The towering oak trees lined the entrance. They swayed gently in the wind as if they were welcoming her to her temporary home. It was a huge building that housed 150 or so women going through a life transition. I brought her some duffle bags and luggage so that she could feel civilized and not have to use supermarket plastic bags for her belongings. I even bought her a few Yoga outfits and nightgowns for her new home.

"Journey, I can't thank you enough for all that you've done for me. You are like the daughter I never had." She bit her quivering bottom lip as tears rolled down her face.

"Ooooh, Janet, don't cry." I hugged her.

"You made me feel like a person, like a whole person. Like I mattered. I will always love you for that."

"Love you too, girl. Don't worry about it. You've helped me in soooo many ways. No one else understands me like you. My mother would never want to know that I have this gift."

"You can't tell people. They will lock you up or be afraid of you."

"I know . . . I know."

"You young and still got plenty of life to live. Now me . . . You know I don't fool with people too much. Just makes it easier."

"Well, this place is gonna be so good for you to help you get back on your feet. They even have a job placement program, and I got you your own personal room." I tapped my temple.

"Oh no, you didn't."

"Oh yes, I did. You said not to abuse it. I used my powers for good. Somehow, they found a vacancy for you."

"Ah shit, I done created a little monster." She laughed a deep, hearty laugh. She held both of my hands. "Okay, now, I'm still gonna come to Yoga on

Sundays. Don't you forget about me. You helped get the kinks outta these old bones and whatnot. I've been feeling so good. So much clearer. Feeling like my old self again." She looked around the isolated parking lot surrounded by trees. "I'm not near our Starbucks no more, and my bike is at my sister-in-law's house now. But I am gonna be there every Sunday. The bus goes right there."

"I can come get you sometimes too. Love you, Janet. Tell Earl to hush up and let you be." We hugged one last time, and my eyes welled up with tears.

"No, Earl is happy I'm gonna be off them streets." She walked toward the entrance and waved.

"See you Sunday."

"Bye, pretty girl."

We kept our secret, and getting to know her changed something in me.

After being on the street for seven years, she started to change her life around. Within three months, she was doing much better. Janet was losing weight, her skin was glowing, and her smile was wider. The shelter had her focused on holistic living. Her diet changed from Burger King, McDonald's, and Checkers to wraps, soups, and salads with my guidance. We were each other's teachers. She came to my free Sunday Yoga classes religiously, and we'd stop by Starbucks after and say hello to Santiago over some tea. It was our Sunday ritual. However, after three weeks of not hearing from her, I felt something was wrong. So I went to the shelter to find her. The receptionist was an older lady who seemed a bit bored. She was knitting a scarf while she watched the door.

"Hello, how may I help you today?"

"Oh yes, I'm here to see Janet. She's in room 203."

She looked in a binder and scanned the list with her finger. "Oh my . . . Oh dear. Yes . . . Janet. Miss Janet." She tilted her glasses down and looked up at me as she picked up a little card from her desk.

"I'm so sorry, hon." She handed me the card.

I covered my mouth. "What? What is this?" I did a double take at the card with an unfocused gaze, then became light-headed.

"We didn't have your number on file. We had a little memorial service for Janet last week."

"Noooo . . . noooo . . ."

"She died suddenly from cirrhosis of the liver two weeks ago. She started losing weight and feeling weak. We found out she was stage four. Then she went to the emergency room and never made it back."

My hands shook as I looked at the card again and just burst into tears. Janet was so young and beautiful in the picture. "Why didn't anyone call me? I mean, I came to get her every Sunday."

"We didn't have your number on file. She had her sister-in-law as the emergency contact."

I sighed. My heart started to hurt. I felt like it was all a bad dream. I couldn't believe it. "I can't believe she's gone. Not my Janet. Shit. I just saw her a few weeks ago." The tears of shock poured off me.

The lady came from behind the receptionist's desk with some tissues for me and hugged me. I just let it all out, sobbing on a stranger.

She rubbed my back. "I'm so sorry, honey. She was a beautiful soul. They had a nice memorial service for her. She was cremated."

"I didn't even know she was sick."

"Apparently, in prior years, she abused alcohol pretty badly, and it took its toll on her body." The receptionist continued rubbing my back.

I was heartbroken. I felt like the world was spinning, and I had to slow my pace as I walked to my car. When I got in, I just let it all out and wept. I mean, I just saw her. She looked fine. She lost weight, and I thought it was because she was eating healthier, walking, and doing Yoga. However, she was most likely dropping weight because of her illness.

One thing that did make me smile is knowing she and Earl would be together now. She was only 53 years old. I'm glad that she could have her own room and be off the streets at least in her last few months of life. That was the least I could do for her in exchange for all she'd given me. I can't lie. I was devastated for a while. Losing Janet was such a shock. It broke me to my core. I hated that I didn't get to say goodbye to one of my best teachers. I vowed to honor her in some way. At first, it was to start a fund to help other homeless women, but then that grew into my whole lifestyle center idea.

Janet profoundly changed my life. Before I got to know her, I just saw her as some crazy person who fucked up her life with drugs. She shifted my beliefs. I knew that with the money I made on the side, I would save it to build my center and donate back to that shelter that helped her and even add to my own future savings. The whole experience was so deep that it made me realize that *I was special* and not to put all homeless people in the "loser" or "drug addict" box.

At first, I thought about calling my center the "New Journey Lifestyle Center," but my spirit urged me to change it to "*A Place for Janet Lifestyle Center.*" It just felt right. Many have even offered to invest in the project. I would love it if my center helped lower-income families and even homeless people in transition, people who really need the services but can't gain access to them. I know once I finalize my business plan and present it, I'll get people to drop major coins without hesitation. Watch. Picture it . . . A beautiful Yoga studio, 3,000 square feet, two enormous rooms for Yoga, and four small offices for massage therapists, chiropractors, and Reiki healers to rent. I wanna be financially free, so even if I'm not teaching, cash will be rolling in. I want to open it downtown. It's a perfect location for all of those who need healing. Of course, I'm talking in the hood too, where it's not yet gentrified.

When I researched Ty and saw he was into real estate, I was beyond happy. I mean, what are the odds? It was a *sign*. I manifested a millionaire real estate developer as my daddy? You can't make this shit up. I've been helping others, and the universe continues to bless me. Of course, I will not ask Ty for any money . . . well, not just yet. I will get to know him more and see how he really feels. I have a good feeling about it all. It's destined. How could he say no to me? I know with men like him, catering to the ego is all I need to do.

Chapter 3

Ty

I was the only child of two immigrants. My mother was from Cuba, and my dad was Jamaican. Failure was not an option in my family. Hard work, sweat, tears, and pride are what my family heritage was built on. Although immigrants, we lived a pretty comfortable middle-class lifestyle. Our home was a modest four-bedroom, two-car garage home—the American dream. I had it in my mind since I was young that I would build a legacy to make my family proud. Even though I had a lot of pressure on me, I also had a huge chip on my shoulder as well. My mother made it her job to build me up, and some might say even coddle and spoil me. She used to call me her *Principito*—her little Prince. I hated when she did it in front of people. My father, on the other hand, was the complete opposite. He always tried to "toughen me up" and had almost a military-style way of parenting. I kept trying to prove that I was worthy of his love, but it was not easy.

Even with all of that, I was an anomaly—a child prodigy, if you will. But after going toe-to-toe with others even smarter than I, I've learned to humble myself over the years. During my teens, I focused on the books and even slowed down with the young ladies. It worked since I scored at the top of my class on the SATs. I was one of the lucky ones to intern at Goldman Sachs with some fantastic mentors. They were impressed with my go-getter attitude and enthusiasm to learn more. They instilled in me that if I continued on this path, I would be a top banker at their investment firm. They said I would clear $250K a year if I stayed on top of my game, and they were right. I did that and then some.

I really had no choice but to grind for success. For starters, back in college, I was flat broke. Most of my school was paid for in academic scholarships. However, I had to make extra money to help my parents with the mortgage and other bills. The Cuban side of my family attained a lot of wealth over the years. In 1965, after the Cuban Revolution, Castro finally allowed people to leave the island. All the money I heard they had was gone by the time I came around. They landed in Miami first, then made their way to Atlanta in the early eighties. My dad left Jamaica in the seventies to attend school in Miami, and that's how he and my mom met.

They all came to the US for a better way of life, but it was not as easy as they had hoped. I was the first to be born in America but not the first to go to college. The men in my family were highly educated, with prominent careers back in Cuba and Jamaica. They all just had to take major downgrades when coming here. Since I was 15 years old, I had to step in to help with some bills. It didn't matter if it was a paper route, mowing lawns, babysitting, or assisting people in moving. I had to earn my keep. So I did whatever I could to make extra money while keeping up with my schoolwork.

My mom and dad constantly bickered over it. Of course, Mom felt my father worked me too hard, and my dad said she was turning me into a pussy. It was bad enough in his eyes that I was a pretty boy that looked and acted nothing like him. I had my mother's caramel skin and curly black hair. So, he did everything he could to toughen me up to make me a "real man." But it did nothing but push me away. It's like nothing I did was good enough. At times, I even felt he was jealous of me, especially of the attention my mom would give me. His tough love was more like verbal abuse, but I learned to live with it. That was his dysfunctional way of showing me love. Sadly, we bumped heads until the day he died in that accident. He was arguing with me until his last breath.

I'll admit, all that hard work turned me into a bit of a nerd. I guess that's why I became so girl-crazy later in life. I always worked or studied during my youth since my parents didn't allow me the freedom most of my American friends had. So it was schoolwork, housework, piano lessons, and side jobs, in that order.

I learned from my mentors that you must spend money to make money. They also stressed that image was everything. I realized that I had to *fake it until I made it*. I knew I needed more clothes, suits for my internship, a nice watch, shoes, and more, but my car—that is all I kept dreaming about. I had my eyes set on this beautiful gold Lexus at the used car dealership in my neighborhood.

I was stepping into the big leagues and wanted a decent car that didn't overheat after fifty miles. I couldn't ask my parents for anything. I was sick of borrowing their car when my hooptie broke down. They had enough troubles. So, coming up with ways to make extra money was my thing. I picked up various side hustles like tutoring high school students. That helped, but it wasn't quite enough. Then one day, one of my classmates told me they got paid $1,000 to $2,000 a month by donating his sperm. He said a few of his friends do it to make extra money. It sounded crazy as hell at first, but then I thought that was an easier route than continuing to slave away at two jobs to make ends meet. It was not coincidental that the sperm banks set up shops near universities. I learned later that it was an actual strategy. We were the perfect target market—smart and broke.

I'm almost embarrassed to admit it, but I thought back then as a 20-year-old that it would be a great idea to share my genes with the world—clone myself. I figured my genes could help make another brilliant mind. I really had an ego on me. I had no genuine idea of what it meant to bring a life into the world. But I was up for it since I wouldn't have to take care of the kid.

Unlike what I told Journey, no one in my family knew. *Not a soul.* Are you kidding me? My mom would have killed me, and my dad would have tortured me, disowned me, *then* killed me. That was a secret I planned on taking to the grave. Only my best friend Marlon knew the truth.

The day I first went to New Life Fertility Group's offices, I had just come from football practice and had to do a swift Superman change in my car. I looked in my rearview mirror, took off my Falcons' baseball cap, and switched out my Notorious B.I.G. shirt to a white shirt and tie with slacks and shiny shoes. If there's one thing my father did teach me, it was how to clean up nicely and be presentable. He always said, "Son, you never get a second chance for a first impression." I was a bit intimidated too since I researched that only 10–15 percent pass all the screenings, so I had to stand out.

My nerves were a wreck. I was sweating so much that I hoped I didn't look like I just ran a mile when I got there. I walked briskly into the high-rise glass building that gave me an intimidating feeling with its futuristic architecture, tall windows, and marble floors. These people definitely had class, and I told myself that I wanted to own a building like that one day. I guess selling sperm was a gold mine for them. I hoped it would be for me too.

The counselor that came to greet me for my appointment was an attractive white lady who looked like she was in her late 30s. She had long, red hair, glasses, and a tight, knee-length skirt. If I didn't know better, I would think she was flirting with me the way she smiled and kept looking at me over her glasses. She was like a sexy schoolteacher. I, however, kept my cool and played the role. I was going to keep it professional.

"Well, good afternoon, Mr. Carter." She looked me up and down. "My, my, you are very well dressed for a college student. You didn't have to do that for me." She pointed to her very lovely breasts. She exuded femininity. I liked her red nails, and she smelled good too.

I chuckled. "Well, I like to be presentable, Mrs. . . ." I tried to read her name tag, but her long hair was covering it.

"Oh, it's Miss Martina O'Reilly, not married." She winked. "Please, have a seat." She had the poise of a dancer. When she sat up extra straight, it accentuated her breasts. I felt like she was doing it on purpose, and I wondered how many of these donors she tried to sleep with. It was pretty obvious she was a horny older lady. I just smiled and played along.

She started pulling up a file on her computer and said, "Well, Mr. Carter, we at—"

I waved my hand to get her attention. "Please, please, call me Ty."

She said in a sultry voice, "Oh, Ty, that's nice. Okay, so, Ty, we at the New Life Fertility Group are so grateful for your interest. So many families have issues conceiving, and many single women would love to have a child but do not have a mate. Being a donor is so needed now, especially with a shortage of . . . well . . . ethnic sperm."

I smirked. "Oh, ethnic, huh?"

"Well, truth be told, traditionally, there are mainly Caucasian women looking for donors. But thanks to the internet taking off with sharing so much information, the popularity of donors has picked up tremendously. Sperm is in high demand for women of all races now. There are many women of color looking for donors, and you seem to have a very diverse background, one might even deem as exotic." She did air quotes for "exotic."

My eyebrows raised. I nodded and tried not to laugh.

"And, Ty, if you qualify after our series of tests, you can make up to at least $1,000 a month, even $1,500 in some cases. We also will give you free health screenings every three months to make sure you are in the best of health. And the best part is it's only five hours a month that we'll need your services."

"Five hours for $1,500 a month sounds good to me."

"Would you like to be contacted after the child turns eighteen?"

"Oh, wow, they can do that?"

"Yes, it's totally up to you. You have the option to remain anonymous, or you can be an ID Disclosure Donor. That just means you'll keep us up to date with your contact information yearly so that we can reach you when the time comes. It's up to you how you want to build a relationship with the child. Your donor sperm will be a little more expensive since they'll have that option to reach you. Just make sure you check that box on the form." She shuffled some papers together and attached them to a clipboard.

"Okay, I'll be in the high-class sperm category then." We both laughed.

"Not so fast. You must be approved first. Take some time to fill out these forms. And then we'll send you to the lab to do some initial testing."

She leaned in more than needed, giving me a peek at her creamy cleavage, and slid a clipboard across the desk with over twenty forms attached to it.

"Take your time and fill them out to the best of your ability. I'll be back for you in an hour."

"Wow, an hour."

"Yes, they are double-sided forms. There are a lot of questions. So, take your time."

"I hope I get accepted, Miss O'Reilly." This time I did add in a little more base in my voice.

She tilted her head and winked. "Oh, I hope you do too. I'm rooting for you, Ty." She rubbed my shoulder on her way out the door, leaving a light scent of her perfume lingering in the air.

Shit, what did I get myself into? I felt like I was about to take a damn exam. My nerves started to get to me. My top lip began to sweat. My hands were shaking slightly as I started filling out the family history. But I needed that money, so I had to man up with the quickness. I had a good feeling Miss O'Reilly wanted to see me again, so she would make sure I got accepted. I figured a little light charm to throw her way couldn't hurt. I did have a way with people. Sometimes, I was amazed at how I could turn situations around in my favor just thinking about it.

Nowadays, they call it the law of attraction, but I thought maybe I just had good luck and then some.

After a month of extensive background checks and psychological evaluations, I was approved. I started to research more about the company and saw letters from thankful families who were so grateful for the service on their website. It made me excited that I would help create a whole human being. I was okay with checking the box for them to contact me since I felt it was important for people to know where they come from.

The money started rolling in, and I was sometimes contributing $500 or more to the household. One day, I gave my mom $500 in cash for the mortgage, and she was so happy, she shed a tear. I went to the bathroom and overheard her tell my dad. He didn't realize I could hear them.

"He gave you this? Maaaan, that boy must be selling drugs or someting. Where he get so much money?"

"Aye, papi, you see the boy is never home. He's always working and tutoring. He's trying to help, and when he does, you complain about that too." I heard a pot slam into the sink. "You are so ridiculous." The water turned on, and Mom sounded like she was washing dishes.

My father said, "Nah, sah, someting ain't right. He's getting all this money, and he not working that hard. Him out there galavanting in the streets with his Lexus, showing off."

"Galavanting? He's working all the time, Carl. He uses his brain. His work doesn't always have to be out in the field, sweating. You should know that, Mr. Accountant. You claim to be at work all hours of the fucking night."

"Ah, shut up ya mouth, woman. You always starting something."

I slammed the bathroom door loud so that they could hear.

My father had the money fanned in his hand and waved it. "Aye, boss man. Where you get all this money from?"

"Hey, Dad, my tutoring gigs. I thought you guys needed it for the mortgage."

"No, we need for the water bill and light bill ya run up. But, tanks. Good work, son."

My mother smiled at me and rolled her eyes at him.

"You're welcome." I shrugged and went to my room. He really made me sick sometimes.

My mother whispered, "You see, he probably heard you."

My dad just sucked his teeth like he couldn't care less.

We never really had money issues until a few years before, when I was about 15. My mom had been doing a lot since my dad lost his big corporate job at the accounting firm some years ago. My mother was a music teacher at a high school and also taught music on weekends. Dad did taxes and accounting for some local businesses, but it didn't bring in nearly as much as he used to. The clients were not consistent, and he was no longer a six-figure earner, but we still had six-figure bills. It was a real hush-hush topic at my house. He had almost made a partner at the accounting firm that he worked for over ten years.

The story on how he got "laid off" was all a lie. Word got out that he was fucking one of the clients. They never told me, but I overheard my mom gossiping with her friend on the phone one day. She was furious, and it didn't sound like it was the first time, either. I stood close to the doorway and hid behind the wall as she sat in the dining room.

"He got himself fired. He said he was laid off, such a fucking liar. The girl called me. Yes, la puta has the nerve to call meeee. I can't believe it, but I knew his ass was not working all that time. Apparently, she left her husband and wanted him to leave me too. He's an idiot. Now, I gotta deal with all these bills. This is the last time. I can't do it anymore—Yes, I keep trying to forgive him, but it's so hard." My mother just started blowing her nose and crying. She was trying to talk through her tears. "He . . . He just keeps denying shit to my face, saying it was a misunderstanding or that the client was lusting after him. I know—Can you

believe his ego? Aye, Betsy, I'm so tired. I would have left him if it weren't for Tyler. He needs a man around, his padre."

I came from out of my hiding space. I couldn't take Mama's tears anymore. It was so hard to hear her cry. "Ma, what's wrong?" I put my hand on her shoulder.

"Look, Betsy, I gotta go, chica." She hung up the phone and looked at me as she wiped her eyes. "Tylercito, it's okay, papi."

"No, it's not okay. What's going on, Mom? You can tell me," I pleaded with a gentle voice.

"Your father lost his job."

"Oh no. Why?" I pretended to be shocked.

"Oh, some disagreement with the partners at the firm. Don't worry, baby, he's looking for another job, but until then, it's just our savings and my income we will live off of, but we'll manage. I'll need a bit more help around the house."

"I can get a job. I can help, you know." I sat down across from her and held her hand.

"Nooo, no, papi. You focus on school, piano lessons, and basketball. You don't have time to work."

"I can tutor on weekends to the younger kids."

She sighed as if giving in. "Well, that's an idea. Only if your schoolwork is done and you can keep up your grades. We'll see."

***

"We'll see" started a major tutoring side hustle for me. My mother already worked with many students in school teaching music, so she would refer new business to me. I was making pretty decent money for a teenager, but it mostly went back into the house for bills. It still wasn't enough, though, and then a few years later is when I started making my weekly "deposits" at The New Life Fertility Group.

One night, I was in my room jamming. I was rapping in the mirror to a Notorious B.I.G. song. I pointed to the mirror rattling off the lyrics to "Nasty Boy." I loved that damn beat. I bumped up the beat a little louder and pretended I was on stage. I was dancing and looking at my fresh haircut. My barber lined me up so tight. I got my first check and was feeling myself. That was the easiest grand I ever made. I was so happy thinking about things I would buy, and I could not wait to give my mom some money. I thought I was helping, but it was just building up tension between my father and me since I knew how he *really* lost his job. He seemed to resent me for stepping up and being a man. I didn't care. Any respect I had for him was gone.

***

I was shaken out of my groove when I heard yelling. At first, I thought it was just their usual yelling, but I turned down my music and heard things being thrown. It sounded like chaos outside my bedroom door.

"You are gonna stop disrespecting me, Carl! You keep putting your dirty dick in everyone else instead of your wife. Soy tu esposa, tu unica esposa. Quieres follarte a esa puta."

"Watch your bloodclot tone with me, Milagros. I don't even know what you are saying. Stop cussing me before I smack the shit outta you."

"I'm sick of it, Carl. Sick of you." A blood-curdling scream escaped her lungs, followed by loud bangs and the sound of shattered dishes. "I'm gonna cut that thing off of you. You let that bitch in here? I swear if you brought her here, I will burn that fucking bed."

I jumped up and ran out of the room to find my mother against the wall and my father holding her there by the throat. A few broken dishes were on the floor.

I screamed, "What are you doing? Get off her!" I tried to pull him back—and he punched me dead in my jaw.

My first instinct was to punch back. I caught him in the eye and then became terrified.

"What the ras? You mussa mad? Boy, you stay out of grown folks' business." He kicked me hard in my leg and stomach like I was some thug in the street and not his child.

My mother screamed, "Get off of him! Leave him! Leave him alone. ¡Ese es tu hijo! What is wrong with you?" She cried with so much pain and pounded on his back with her tiny fists, but it did nothing to him.

I sat up on the floor, holding my throbbing jaw in shock. His eyes were bloodshot red, and his nostrils flared. We were both so afraid of him. My father never hit me like that. I had spankings as a kid, but he never punched me. I think because I was taller than him now, he was scared too.

I stood up. "Leave Mom alone. What's wrong with you, Dad?"

"What's wrong with me? She had a fucking knife, Ty. A goddayaamn knife." Sweat dripped off of his face. He spoke out of breath, "She lucky I don't kill her dead right now!" He just shoved me out of the way, walked out, and slammed the door behind him. I looked on the floor and saw a big steak knife lying there. I guess she just had it to scare him. I couldn't see her really using it.

My mom ran over to me to check my face. "Aye, you're bleeding. Mi principito estás bien. ¿Estás herido?" She got a wet rag from the kitchen and put some ice on my face. As she was catering to me, I saw the red handprints on her neck, which made me more furious.

That was it for me. I was done with him.

"Mom, he can't stay here. He can't put his hands on you. He could have killed you. He hit and kicked me like I was a damn burglar or something. He's not right in his head. He's losing it."

I got my wish, at least temporarily. He stayed in a hotel that night, but he came back as if nothing ever happened the next day. I hated the way my mom always put up with his bullshit. I felt like he probably abused her before, and they just hid it from me. Once I knew the truth about him, our relationship got worse. We barely spoke. I was still respectful, but I tried not to spend any time with him, and it was apparent. He didn't even try to make it right because he knew he fucked up, and there was no way I could ever look up to him again with respect.

I felt like he hated me at times. Especially after that blow to his ego. My mom would say, "Tyler is more of a man of this house right now." Then I realized that just because someone is blood doesn't mean you can trust them or even have to love them. I was determined to be a better man than him, and if I ever were to be a father, I would not be anything like him.

***

After six months of "working" for The New Life Fertility Group and my fifteenth deposit, I was all caught up with bills. I had purchased my shiny, *almost new* gold Lexus and even threw my hat into the ring and bought some stocks. I knew my father was jealous that I had a better car than he did, and I guess it was my way of rubbing it into his face that I could help with bills and *still* get the car of my dreams. It did make me look like money, and that's when my career took off. Money was so good that I moved on and forgot all about being a donor until the day I got the call asking me if I was #1544.

Chapter 4

Journey

For almost a year, I studied Ty before I could muster up the courage and go through with contacting him. I was still pretty much in shock, to be honest. You would think my mother would have found a smoother way of telling me the truth, but she decided to introduce me to my father the way a coward would. She danced around it. I had just come home from taking a Yoga class and was blowing out my hair. Then I saw her reflection behind me in the doorway.

I turned off the dryer. "What's up, Mom?"

"When did you get that wooden Buddha with the rhinestones in it?" She walked into my room and touched it. "Oh, it's a candleholder. That smells good."

"Natalia got it for me on my birthday."

"What's that scent?"

"Vanilla and citrus." I looked at her poking around on my dresser. She was nervous about something. It didn't help that I was a little high from some edible honey I had with my tea earlier, so I hoped she didn't notice. I think it was making me more paranoid of her coming into my room to chitchat about nothing.

"I wish you didn't shave off that side of your hair." She sulked and pushed her long, curly hair behind her ears.

"You still on this? It'll grow back. Stop worrying about it." I shook my head and smiled.

She sighed and stared at me. It was starting to creep me out. "Listen, Nini, I have something to tell you." She sat on my bed and patted the spot next to her. I sat next to her, and she handed me a printout of a baby picture. It looked kind of old. It was a black-and-white photocopy. The eyes of the baby were big. He was smiling so happily.

"Who is this?" I looked closer at the photo and could tell the baby was a little boy. He had on a little bow tie and was adorable. I felt a jolt. An uneasy feeling was coming from my mom. "Who is this, Mommy? A cousin or something?" She started fidgeting, and I felt the anxiety coming from her. I shouted at her in my mind, What is it? Tell me now. What are you hiding? The words never came out of my mouth, but she jumped up as if she heard them.

"Mom, why are you looking at me like that? You're scaring me."

She lowered her gaze and shook her head. "Nini, I never wanted to tell you since I didn't want you to grow up feeling like an outcast or awkward, but this little boy . . . He's, ah, he's your father."

"I thought you said you had no photos of him."

"I didn't. I had to call and get it."

"Call? Call who? And what does that have to do with being an outcast?"

"It's a long story, but you know with my condition, tomorrow is not promised. I don't know how much longer I'm going to be around. Doctors think it is some rare form of an autoimmune disease. I don't want to scare you, but you should know I'm waiting for some more results to come back from my blood work."

My heart dropped. "Don't say that. Stop talking like that. You're in remission, and you'll be fine. You'll be fine."

"Well, you know it can come back. I just want to make sure you know you are not alone. Your father . . . Well, I do not know him personally."

"What? What the hell do you mean?"

"Watch your mouth." She sighed, "Everyone I knew had their families, and I wasn't getting any younger, Journey. By the time I hit thirty-nine, I knew I wanted a baby, and time was slipping away from me. I was considered a high risk at my

age. I didn't find a good partner, so I decided to do it alone."

I got up and started pacing back and forth. I was anxious and angry. "With a stranger? Soooo, all of these stories about him moving on after a short fling, all of those stories about him starting a new family in Cali . . . Was that all lies?"

She nodded shamefully, and tears in her eyes grew as she cupped her mouth. Her face became red.

I pointed at her. "So, you think allowing me to grow up feeling so unwanted with abandonment issues was better?" I held my hands up in the air. "Who does that, man? That's my father? What's his name?"

"Well, I didn't know how to tell you the truth. I figured you wouldn't try to find him if you felt that he moved on. I know, it wasn't right."

I took a deep breath, and a tear rolled down my face. My chest tightened. I didn't know what a panic attack felt like, but my body sure was reacting.

"You're old enough now." She sighed. " And yes, your father is alive. He was a donor to help me conceive you through insemination. Please forgive me, Nini. I'm so sorry I held this from you." She tried to hold my hand, but I shrugged her off.

"You're sorry you held this from me? Do you mean you're sorry that you lied? I . . . I can't be-

lieve you. Are you freaking serious?" I felt a lump in my throat. My stomach was in knots.

Her voice was a faint whisper. "Yes, and he lives right here in Atlanta. I found him, and he's a successful businessman. The sperm bank I used had photos on the site and—"

My eyes widened. "Wait. This is a lot to unpack. So, like a sperm donor?"

"Yes, I know it sounds crazy, but it was very modern, even back then. The company had full bios on donors with baby pictures of them so you could get an idea of what they looked like. I chose him because he was an honor student all his life. He had a great mind. He was a beautiful brown child with Latino lineage. He was tested for everything. The company did a comprehensive background screening on donors. Psych evaluations and all. I think that's why you are so talented and smart. When he donated, he checked the box that said that after you turned eighteen, you could contact him. That was the agreement he signed."

I turned my back to her and looked out the window. I didn't even want to look at her. I was disgusted. "Come on—please, tell me you're joking. This is so messed up. This is freaking crazy. Are you trying to get me back from April Fool's Day?" I laughed. "This was genius. You're getting better." I wagged my finger at her. "Am I being punked?" I looked around for a camera and wiped my eyes, hoping it was all a big joke for social media.

"No, baby. I know you're going to be mad at me for a while, but I want you to know him, connect with him. I have the number to call him."

"I can't believe you hid this from me. That's just so wrong to do that, Mommy. Dead wrong." I walked off, went into the den, and slammed the door. I pushed some of her books off the desk and kicked a chair on its side. I was so mad I wanted to punch her, but I just cried into the couch pillow instead.

It all made sense now. I always felt like something was missing in my life. I felt rejected, thrown away. I felt my dad did not want me. I never realized it, but my "daddy issues" have really affected me over the years. Most of my recent boyfriends have been older men. I also got a kick out of controlling older men in general, even in Yoga. It gave me back my power.

But *this* shit was so unexpected. My mom could never keep a man, and quite frankly, I don't think she ever really wanted one. She was always so driven and focused on being the best. More focused on what people thought. Trying to be "Miss Fucking Perfect" all her life. I was sure that my father was tired of her shit and just left. I was a mixed stew of emotions. Betrayal, anger, resentment, and happiness all rolled into one. Thrilled to know I had a father who was alive and willing to meet me.

As furious as I was, I had to admit that I was afraid my mom's illness would take over again too. I was angry that she didn't take care of herself enough and ended up sick. I was pissed that she could lie to me all these years. I mean, yeah, it was a weird thing to tell a kid, but it was not that uncommon. I just know she's terrified of dying and leaving me alone because it seems as if she would have never told me otherwise. That's the real fucked-up part.

After that, my mother walked around the house on eggshells, trying her hardest to make my favorite Colombian meals like bandeja paisa and empanadas. I tried to avoid her since I was still so furious. We didn't speak for a few days, and finally, I asked for his full name and number. Then the research began.

When I think back on that day she told me, I understood why she picked Ty. Aside from him being chosen like a lab rat because of his intelligence. I'm sure she picked him because he was brown-skinned. My abuela in Colombia was a low-key racist. My mom told me stories about when she would date a Black man, and her mother would say he looked like a monkey with curly hair or some racist remark and laughed. I know my mother wished I came out even darker than my mocha-brown complexion just to spite her bigoted relatives. However, I think my melanin did its job since they tormented me for it during my childhood. I'm very proud of my skin now, but summers in Colombia were not always fun. I was told to stay out of the sun before I got too black. I was teased a lot by kids because I was different, and my Spanish wasn't that great either. The girls were mean, and the boys that did like me called me "*Negrita.*" I didn't mind the nickname since they said it with love, and it just meant little brown girl.

I think having haters, especially jealous females since I was a kid, is why, for the most part, I have been a loner. I get along with guys much better. I think my mom thought I was too much of a tomboy and probably was afraid I was gonna "turn gay" or something. My heart chakra was just pretty blocked, and it gave me an edge and made me probably intimidating to some.

Natalia is pretty much the only one I let get close to me recently. I have my homegirls from Yoga training, but I keep shit light with them. They don't really *know me-know me*. In the last six months, I formed a group of friends online who are exploring their gifts like me. It's been my biggest attempt to come out of my cave and be open to making deeper connections. We talk almost every day, and it feels good to know I'm not alone going through a spiritual awakening. I named our group "The Fantastic Four" since we joke around about us being superheroes or magicians. We do little games each day to test our abilities, and so far, it seems to be helping us all. Not to brag, but it looks like Robbie and I are the most skilled in the group.

Robbie is a brother who is an empath/medium from the Bronx. He has prophetic dreams and can see auras. He might be even better than all of us.

Elizabeth is a Mexican chick from Cali who is into healing arts like Reiki and body talk. She is also pretty psychic as well.

Zack is a hipster white boy with blond dreads who is good at remote viewing. He's in Colorado. You can give him a location, and he can see what's there.

And me—well, I'm rather good with psychic abilities, telepathy, and I'm working on improving my out-of-body experiences. It's the coolest thing when you can see your body in the bed and feel yourself floating. It freaked me out the first couple of times, but I'm now learning to control it.

We are all close in age, between 20 and 24. Since I started the group, they kinda look up to me to lead. I love being in charge, so it works out.

I called them up on video chat, and, as usual, Zack looked high as hell. He is a true stoner and gets the good stuff from Colorado. His stepdad owns a dispensary and some clinics nationwide. His family is filthy rich. His room looks like a damn hotel suite. I couldn't wait until we all went to visit him.

Elizabeth has just finished studying some new psychology courses. She wants to be a therapist. She's really into school, the nerd of the group.

Robbie was outside in the park and just finished playing ball. "Yo, what up, what up?" he said with his chocolate face dripping in sweat. "I just finished dunking on these suckers."

I asked in my teacher's voice, "That's nice, but did y'all do the exercise?"

Elizabeth said, "Yes, I got blue socks."

Robbie yelled, "I saw a kitten or cats. I don't know what the hell that was." He laughed.

Zack scratched his golden locks. In a slow, Midwestern drawl, he said, "Shit, I didn't get any of that. I just saw a gray blanket. I felt like I was melting in my bed. It was pretty heavy, but I was microdosing on shrooms so—"

"You stay high, Zack," I said. We all laughed.

"But y'all are not ready for the answer. I am like, holy shit." I jumped up and screamed. "You were *all* right. Last night, I had on blue socks, and my pajama pants had kittens on them."

Elizabeth tilted her glasses into the screen. "Kittens? I thought you were much cooler, Journey."

"Shut up, Elizabeth," I laughed. "But check this out. Here's the crazy part. I had my gray weighted blanket on me. Here's why I think you felt me melting in the bed, Zack." I aimed my camera on the bed to show them.

"Whaaaat?" they all yelled in unison.

I calmly smiled. "I don't know why you guys are so shocked. We all have it. We are the fucking X-Men, I tell ya. I got an idea. Tonight, we do my house and see if you can visit around the same time. Let's say eleven p.m. EST. We can check results tomorrow."

"Like remote viewing. What Zack does? I don't know . . ." Elizabeth shrugged.

"Yes, you can do it, girl. Just try to get at least three things. I'll text y'all the address."

"Copy," Robbie said.

"Talk to you guys tomorrow."

"Over and out," Zack mumbled.

Knowing you have abilities is one thing, but having a tribe to share it with and practice with makes it so much more rewarding. When I open A Place for Janet Lifestyle Center, I'm definitely going to have metaphysical courses. I love practicing because the more I do, I can really get whatever I want out of life. Psychic abilities are even better than college. I can create my school and master how to control this gift. I am already surprisingly good, but I know I'm about to get even better. I studied daily and read books by and about psychics like James Van Praagh, Edgar Cayce, Johanne Rutledge, Echo Bodine, Denise Hinn, and Robert Monroe. These are my teachers in *my* university, a.k.a. my library. I'm going to get the best teachers to come to my center too.

My mom always said I was a bit too woo-woo, and I needed to come down to earth. She wasn't even crazy about me being a Yoga teacher at first since she saw me having less interest in school. She is so linear and lives in a world of logic, facts, and stats. For someone so brilliant, she didn't understand that intuition is the next level of intelligence. The unexplainable or things with a mystical influence were just too much for her to grasp. She didn't want to believe that humans can use their sixth sense to the level that we do. I got a vibe from her once that she did believe, but she was just afraid of it. She might even be scared of me since she knows I see more than she does at times. The intelligent thing to do would be to embrace it to use it in her court cases and get larger settlements for her clients. But nope, I will let her stay right in her little rigid world, and I'll keep elevating in mine.

Chapter 5

Ty

I didn't really get it in my youth, but as I got older, I knew there was a bit more to what I was capable of, and I'm still learning. I used to think I was just a good guesser, but after meeting with Journey, I felt it indeed was the gift of intuition. Of course, I had a little bit more confirmation since she has it too. I always had a great knack for choosing the right stock, finding amazing real estate locations, and, well, I don't mean to toot my own horn, but I had a way with the ladies as well.

Marlon was my best friend for over twenty years and business partner for the last five. He was a no-nonsense dude from Brooklyn, New York, but when it came to fun, the brother was the life of the party. I loved that he knew how to work hard and play hard. But when it comes to business, I usually do not make any financial moves without informing him. We just returned from looking at a new location we're thinking about investing in and decided to have a drink at the bar downstairs from my building.

The vibe was always so chill. Old-school hip-hop music played in the background as the after-work crowd trickled in. The drinks were strong, and the food was good, so it was our little hangout spot.

Marlon took off his hat and blazer while mumbling, "It's hot as fuck in here."

The bartender, Sammy, said, "Well, we just opened. Give it a few for the air to kick in."

Marlon reached for a napkin and patted the sweat on his shiny brown head.

"Yeah, you look like a melting chocolate Milk Dud," I teased.

"Man, shut up. This Atlanta fall weather be tripping. It'll be thirty-seven degrees in the morning and seventy-eight by three p.m. So, um . . . Tell me, how was it, man? Tell me more about the meeting. Did it freak you out meeting your daughter? Your ass musta been so nervous."

"Hell yeah, I was nervous. It was surreal." I sat back and sighed. "I mean, to look at your own flesh and blood. You know I don't want to have kids at this stage in my life, but to see some resemblance of family genes . . . It was pretty amazing. She is beautiful too. I can't believe we forgot to take pictures."

"Oh, I'd love to see her." Marlon seemed very happy for me.

"She's a little rebel, though. Had all these piercings, and she had a sleeve tatt like me—a whole arm, man. She had a real down-to-earth vibe about her. And you know what? She was pretty intuitive."

"Oh, just like her pops then with your old Warlock ass."

"Man, knock it off with that. I mean intuitive, like she was easy to vibe with. Like she gets me. It was like she knew what I would say before I said it. It felt like I was talking with an old friend."

"Like I said—ya Harry Potter ass. You got a little witch daughter. I'ma buy y'all his and hers matching witch hats. You can probably teach her to walk through walls like you. Watch." He pointed at me with his beer.

Since college, Marlon had this running joke: I was a warlock with magical powers, and I was just visiting from another dimension. I did get visions at times, but most of the time, I kept them to myself. I was sick of him teasing me.

"Come on, man, you know I don't walk through no damn walls."

"Yes, the fuck you do, Negroooo. The year was nineteen hundred and ninety-nine." The bartender heard him and laughed. "Whatchu looking at, Sammy?" Marlon cut his eyes playfully at him. "As I said, nineteen hundred and ninety-nine. You was at my house. You was spying on me fucking Brenda in my kitchen wit'cho nosy no-pussy-getting ass."

"Yo, turn down the volume." I blushed. Okay, so I was one of the last virgins in our crew, but I'd made up for the lost time.

"Yo, Ty, you described everything to me like you was there. I swore you were there with binoculars or some shit. You even described her skirt. Those shits you be having are not 'dreams' like you call them. You on some next-level shit."

"It was a lucky guess." I shrugged my shoulders. "But yoooo, you took it back." I started rapping LL Cool J's song, "*Brenda got a big ole butt . . .*"

We sang in unison and just fell out laughing.

"Man, those were the days. Whatever happened to Brenda?"

"Oh, she messed around and got pregnant with two bigheaded twins. 'Memba that big goon nigga from New York that used to come down here to sell coke at AUC parties? He got locked up for life, and she fat as fuck now."

"Oh, okay then." I took a swig of my beer and shook my head.

"So, tell me more about Journey. You see her mom? What she look like?"

"No, I haven't, but she's Colombian."

"Aha. Just how you like 'em."

"Come on, man. I doubt I will be trying to hook up with the mom."

"Well, if your daughter is pretty, Mama probably look good too. So, what else? I need details. Are you guys going to hang out more? Are you gonna step up and be a daddy for real?"

"Nah, I'll just be friends with her. I'm not trying to step into that role. I just think building a friendship with her will be nice. We will probably do lunch or dinner soon. I want to get to know her more. The kid has a good head on her shoulders. Already has investment ideas for a wellness center. She's a Yoga teacher now and goes to SCAD."

"Dope and word? Yoga? I need her to teach me. Maybe she can come down to the office and give us a midday stretch break."

"That sounds like a great idea. I'll run it by her to find out her fee."

"Fee? How about the 'daddy' rate, a.k.a. free."

"Come on; she's a kid trying to make a way for herself."

"All right, all right. You know how we hustle."

"Cheap motherfucker–it's not like we don't have it."

"Yeah, we have 'it,' because *I'm* the CFO, nigga."

"Yeah, yeah," I chuckled. "So, listen–the other big news is we got a new intern. She's Journey's good friend." I took a sip of my beer, preparing for the negative bullshit.

"Ah, come oooon, man. You know we don't want no kids on the team. Remember what happened last year? They were posting all reckless on our social media, typos everywhere. Just a hot mess. They have attention spans of fleas."

"No, no. Not that kind of intern, Marlon. She's grown. Thirty-two years old, to be exact. She's more like a big sister to Journey. But get this. She went to Spelman for business and is working at an insurance firm by day. She's also studying to be a realtor and investor. She's a smart woman. I already hired her temporarily to try her out."

"What? Without consulting *me*, your CFO? She must be fine or something."

"Well, she's an intern, so we're not paying her—yet." I shrugged. "And I can't lie. She definitely has my attention." I smiled.

"Don't do it, maaaan. You know your dick always lands you into trouble. We don't need no crazy bitches in the company *again*." He slammed his hand on the counter, being overly dramatic as usual.

"Nah, nah. I promise to keep it professional, but damn, she is *so* sexy." I tilted my head back, picturing her and her cute, dainty little walk. "She just has a lot of class."

"Is she Spanish, Black, Asian, white?"

I chuckled and shook my head. I looked at him as if he should already know my type.

He leaned in. "Oh, okay, Black? Scale of one to ten?"

"She's at least an eight and a half. Gorgeous skin, great tits, nice legs, and a plump ass. Dresses really classy. Just exudes femininity. She was probably a dancer."

"Oh, *that* explains it."

"No, not an exotic dancer. She carries herself with poise like a ballerina or something."

Marlon patted my back, "Okay, okay, no falling in love with employees, and she's your daughter's friend. Don't be that dirty old man." He raised his eyebrows. "Soooo, ummm . . . That could be a little messy. But I think I'm going to check her out for myself." He rubbed his hands together like an evil villain and laughed.

"Hell no. You stay over there in *your* lane with your white and Asian chicks. Leave the mocha to me."

"Come on, bro, share the love. I still love Black women. They just don't love me. Don't do me like that. You got a lot of fucking nerve with your Latina nurse you smashing every chance you get."

"*Afro*-Latina. She's Dominican and just as Black as us. She just got a little Goya and Sazon sprinkled on that ass." I pretended to sprinkle imaginary seasoning in the air.

He chuckled. "Okay, you right, you right. So, what you got this girl doing exactly? What's her name again?"

"It's Natalia. For now, she's doing some research on some properties; nothing major yet. I want to see how creative a thinker she is, but I think she'll do well in property management. I want to train her in a few areas."

"Okay, send me her résumé. Just don't do your warlock shit on her and have her *and* the nurse fucking you."

"Ah, man, now that would be amazing . . . at the same time?" I closed my eyes to picture it for a second with a big smile on my face. "But come on, man. I don't use powers. I can't help it if I'm a lady magnet." I dusted off my shoulder playfully.

"Magnet, my ass. They want that wallet. *That's* what they want."

"See, you always hating on a brother. Don't be mad at me that you came out of the womb looking like *that*."

"Man, shut the fuck up." We laughed.

Sammy wiped off the counter and picked up some tips. "Wow, you guys are true friends because those are fighting words."

"Maaaan, listen, he don't want none of *this* smoke." Marlon flexed his tiny muscles, and we all just cracked up. He wasn't skinny but had a much-smaller frame than me.

Marlon talking about my little "special talents" reminded me that I am a little bit afraid of my visions. My visions are what first got my ex-wife busted. She told me she was out with "friends" when my vision showed me her deep throating a nigga she met online. Just one of her entanglements that I had to deal with. I was no angel either, but that was the beginning of the end.

I hadn't had many visions lately until I met Journey, but truth be told, I was a bit terrified of them since I didn't have control over them. Then I learned my visions were called out-of-body experiences. I have even seen myself in bed while I floated over my body—creepy shit.

I knew that I was pretty good at being persuasive or projecting my feelings into people's minds to the point of influencing their thoughts. Unfortunately, I did not have a good grasp of how to use my talent, especially related to women. I might have even abused it. I feel guilty thinking about it since I know I was in overdrive back in the day. I had a raging appetite for sex in my 20s. I still do, but it's not as bad. If I wanted to have sex with you, I was going to have sex with you. Don't get me wrong. It's not like rape or anything like that, but my level of confidence got me a lot of girls, and quite frankly, got me into a lot of trouble. Many would call it charm, but I knew there was more to it than that. It was as if my "crazy girl" magnet was at an all-time high. I would have girls becoming so obsessed with me that it truly got out of hand. By the time my Lexus got keyed twice, I had learned my lesson and stopped being a dog. Well, temporarily . . . until I got introduced to polygamy. Then the game changed. I had to be open to take some of my own medicine.

The chill of the elevator's A/C gave my sweaty body goose pimples. I just got in from a five-mile jog in the park. It was a beautiful day too, a perfect seventy-seven degrees. As the elevator doors opened, I could hear the faint sound of salsa coming down the hall from my apartment. As I got closer, I thought the music was much too loud. I mumbled as I opened the door, "You have *got* to be kidding me."

That damn Jocelyn and her after-breakfast parties. I came in, and a Celia Cruz song was playing on level ten. I peeked behind the hallway wall to see Jocelyn dancing salsa by herself. Her curly brown hair bounced when she moved. She was in bright purple scrubs today and getting low to the ground as if she were in a nightclub. Even with scrubs, you can see every voluptuous curve in her body. She was one fine specimen and good at her job too.

Papa was tapping his feet, a little slow and offbeat but engaging, nonetheless. To see him tapping and clapping was good enough for me since he usually just stares into space or at the TV. I couldn't help but smile since his eyes lit up with life. Jocelyn noticed me and started clapping and stomping her feet to the beat as if calling me to join her. I took her hand and spun her around. I did a few salsa steps. You see—I could hold my own, but I was not as good as her. She tapped my hips to encourage me to move them more.

She did a few spins, and I caught her and dipped. Then I said in a loud and stern tone, "Alexa, turn the volume down fifty percent."

Papa yelled clear as day, "No, Tylercitoooo." Jocelyn and I looked at each other in awe.

"Papa, I'm so sorry, but it's too early. We can't be blasting music like that."

Jocelyn walked over to Papa and bent down close to his face. "I know, Señor Garcia, he is a party pooper." She did an exaggerated pout with her lips and looked at me.

"It's ten a.m. on a weekday. You can't be blasting music like it's a summer block party. You want the neighbors to be complaining? I got enough stuff to deal with, Jocelyn."

She rushed into the kitchen. "Aye, so grumpy in the morning. Most people are at work. Why do you care? You *own* the building, Mr. Carter."

"That's beside the point, and no one knows that. That's why I have a property management company."

She opened the fridge and took out my green protein smoothie that she prepared while I was jogging. She took a spoon and stirred it. Jocelyn softened her tone and looked at me with her doe-like eyes. "Okaaaay, I'll keep it down, but you know music is a part of your abuelo's therapy? Music is healing him, especially when I put on music from his younger days. Then he goes insane. Don't you see a change in him? He's more alert when I dance for him."

I snickered. "You're right, but shit, who wouldn't be more alert?" I scanned her body up and down and took a washcloth from my back pocket to wipe off the sweat from my forehead. Then I walked behind her in the kitchen.

Jocelyn took a napkin and wrapped it around my drink. I took the smoothie from her grasp and nodded as I took a sip. We stood close together, and I spoke lower. "I know what made him alert . . . that fat ass you were shaking in front of him. The man is eighty-five. Don't go giving him a heart attack. He hasn't had any pussy in years." I rubbed my hand across her butt, and she giggled.

Jocelyn leaned into my neck. "Whew, you stink." She waved in front of her nose.

"Why don't you come wash it off of me?" I took the last swig of my smoothie and put it in the sink. Then I started to walk away and looked back, expecting her to follow.

She mouthed, "Later . . ." Then whispered, "Wait until he takes a nap. You know he is paying attention, even though he pretends he isn't." She pointed her chin toward Papa.

I shrugged. "Okay." I stood in the hallway smiling and stroked my hardness in my jogging pants. She couldn't take seeing that.

"Okaaaay. Jesus, you make it so difficult for me to do my job."

I started stripping out of my wet tank top as I walked to the bathroom. "This *is* a part of your job," I yelled down the hallway.

"Noooo, it's not. You got the bonus." She raised her voice so he could hear her over the salsa. "Let me bring Papa his tea, and I'll be there in a minute to help you clean up the office."

"That's what I thought," I shouted back and laughed.

I know I shouldn't have, but I have been so immersed in work that I haven't had time to date. My messy divorce became final two years ago, and quite frankly, I didn't want any more drama. Jocelyn fulfills all my needs right now. During the interview process, I turned down many older, motherly-type of women for this beautiful Dominican woman with a lot of sass. I knew Papa would need it, and I can't lie. I just wanted something beautiful to look at. We had an instant attraction, but I did make sure she was highly qualified too. Her looks and personality were definitely a bonus. She takes care of both of us pretty well. I could trust her in my home with him alone when I had to work in the office or leave town.

I was pretty good the first couple of months. We had our light flirting, like brushing up against each other in the kitchen, you know—small things like that. Then one day, I was so horny I couldn't ignore her advances. Now, we seemed to have fallen into a little rhythm. I just try to keep it all at home. We don't go on dates, I don't ask her about her personal life, and she doesn't ask me about mine. It's much better this way—less messy, and it helps avoid chaos. I don't want to give her mixed signals. I haven't wanted a relationship for a while, and I'm not sure when I'll be ready again. It feels good having her around, taking care of Papa and me, so I'll just enjoy it while it lasts.

I started showering, then heard the door crack. I motioned for her to join me.

"No, Ty. My hair is going to get wet. You really think Papa is stupid too, don't you? He'll notice." She started to remove her scrub bottoms slowly, revealing her cocoa-brown thick thighs and purple lace panties. "I'll just watch you." She tilted her head to the side and admired me washing my body.

"Okay, if you can handle it. You know that pussy gets wet fast." I wiped the steam off the glass so that she could get a full glimpse of my soapy body.

"Take that top off. I want to see everything. I'm going to fuck you right there on that chair when I get out." I started to stroke myself, and Jocelyn took off her top very slowly, never taking her eyes off me. Her skin was so beautiful.

She came closer to the glass shower doors and pressed her naked body up against them. "Ooooh, I can't wait to get out of the shower. You're gonna get it," I chuckled. I started to rinse myself off in a hurry. Jocelyn began fondling herself in between her legs and biting her bottom lip. She was such a freak, and I loved it. "Keep playing with me, and I'm going to drag you in here."

"Noooo, Ty, I mean it . . . my hair. I just curled it. It's gonna frizz," she giggled.

I turned off the water, and she took my towel from the hook and started to dry me off. I love how attentive she was and how she loved to serve me like I was royalty. She knew how to treat a man and how to make me feel like a king. Jocelyn gently caressed my hard dick and said, "Oh, it's so nice and clean now."

"Yes, just for you." I loved watching her stroke me.

She got down on her knees, rubbed my thighs, and started to kiss my legs. She worked her way up slowly and started to suck me so damn good. I had to hold myself up against that wall because she came in so powerfully. I wasn't expecting it.

She stroked and sucked me with one hand and reached under the sink for a condom with the other. Jocelyn was a talented woman, for sure.

I pulled her away gently by her hair. “Come here.” I led her to the chair that had my clothes on it. She pushed them to the ground. I quickly rolled the condom on and sat down. She straddled me and began riding me so good.

“Damn, you are so wet . . . This pussy was waiting for me, huh?”

“Yessss . . .” She came down on me slow and gentle. She was so tight, like she practiced Kegels all day.

Jocelyn looked into my eyes as she wound up her waist on my dick real slow and sexy. I sucked on her big, plump breasts as she rode me. She started moaning, “Baby, this shit feels soooo good.”

“Best way to start your day, huh?” I smiled and pushed her hair out of her face as I kissed her. I sped up the pace and started to rock her up and down on me a little harder. My fingers dug deep into her ass.

“Yessss. Yessss. Ouch, not so deep, Ty.”

I groaned. “Come oooon, you can take it,” I whispered in her ear. I slapped her ass. “You’re a big girl. Take this dick.” I went faster and even harder. My pep talk worked since she joined my pace and came down on me hard. She muffled her cries into my shoulder. Even though we were in the back of the house, the large bathroom with marble floors sometimes echoed. The loud sounds of our slapping damp skin turned me on even more and made me explode.

"Ahhh fuck, I'm coming, I'm coming!"

"Would you shush? You so loud, papi," she laughed. She grabbed the back of my neck and kept moving, even though I was paralyzed.

I whispered, "Come oooon. Old man can't hear a thing." I hugged her into me even deeper as I came. She kissed me and started to shiver on me like she was having a convulsion. "You want to get caught, don't you? That shit made you come just thinking about it. I know you want me and Papa at the same time. I saw you shaking that fat ass for him earlier." I giggled into her shoulder.

"Shut up. You're so sick, but oh God, I love your fat dick."

"And I love that fat ass. The Breakfast of Champions." I raised a fist in the air. "You know how to work it, mami."

She rose off me slowly while sucking her teeth. Jocelyn went into the linen closet for a rag to wipe up.

"Okay, that was a nice break. Let me get back to Señor Garcia. That was good, Ty. So good. I mean, Mr. Carter."

"You can call me Ty anytime you want."

She winked at me as she put on her scrubs and went right back into caregiver mode. I love the care that she gives me too. I'm never letting that fine ass go. She gets my day started better than some Jamaican Blue Mountain Coffee.

My day took off full speed ahead with back-to-back meetings. I hopped on a few conference calls with some investors and reviewed a few contracts before taking a quick break. My eyes were killing me from the computer screen. I went into the living room and felt like playing the keys a bit. It relaxed me. "Hey, Papa, let me play a little tune for you. You want to hear 'In a Sentimental Mood'?"

He smiled and said softly, "Sí, sí, Tyler."

Papa loved Duke Ellington.

Jocelyn was in the kitchen drying her hands from washing dishes. "Good timing," she said. "You're just in time for his therapy. I love to hear you play. It's so soothing." She tapped the piano.

I stroked the keys and smiled at them as I played. Jocelyn stood behind Papa and started to stretch his arms in the air and do slow circles to wake them up. We found that music helped make him do his therapy with joy and no fussing. When I played piano, it was as if his gray eyes would light up.

I remember playing piano with Papa on Christmas and Thanksgiving. The house would be packed with family. Those were happier times when my entire family got together. The Cuban side would visit from Miami and the Jamaicans from New York and Fort Lauderdale. The house had the aroma of flavorful spices, and, of course, the food was just amazing. As a kid, I didn't realize how refined my palate was growing up with Jamaican and Cuban heritage. Everyone knew how to throw down in the kitchen, even me, but since Jocelyn's been around, I've let her take over.

My dad would be in the backyard on the grill making jerk wings or playing dominoes with his cousins. Papa would start playing the piano and putting the family in such a good mood. When my fingers danced over the keyboard, it was as if it were my little time machine. I was in a zone, being sucked back into a simpler time of my childhood, a time when I was the star of the show at family gatherings . . . When both sides of my family would be one. My Cuban grandmother, Mercedes, was the entertainer with her beautiful voice, and Papa would play the piano. Together, they performed songs from Nat King Cole, Elvis, Rubén Blades, and, of course, Celia Cruz, whom my abuela idolized. After all, Celia was The Queen of Salsa from Cuba. Then they would always ask me to play a tune of something recently learned. I hated it at first, having all eyes on me since I was a shy kid, but eventually, the attention boosted my ego.

"He's so talented."
"What a bright kid."
"Este chico tiene tremendo talento."
"Tyler is so handsome."

Being in the mix of things, I would overhear them reminiscing over the "glory days," where he got his nickname of Papi Ching-Ching. I miss all of their stories of living in Cuba, how they had so much wealth and a nice home. I loved to see how much Papa adored his wife. They were an example of true love, being married for fifty-four years. Back then, I thought my parents would be just the same. However, fast-forward a decade, and they could barely stand each other. I'm sure my mother stayed for me. They were old-fashioned and didn't believe in divorce. I just hated seeing my mom live a lie and staying in a loveless marriage because she thought she was doing *me* a favor.

Sadly, I think making me stay and watch my dad's philandering ways helped me build some of his bad qualities. I saw how much a woman would put up with. I had a thirst so intense that one woman was never enough. That's why I figured when I met my ex-wife, who was open to polygamy, that all my prayers were answered . . . or so I thought. We dated for one year, and I felt that she was the one, especially since we had a few threesomes, and I knew she was into it. Well, even though we signed up for a polygamous relationship, we didn't follow our own rules. So the fights were never ending. We both were very lustful and had animalistic cravings, so when it was good, it was good. When it was bad, I ended up hiring a detective, and she started tracking my whereabouts with a device she planted in my car. One time, we were even cheating with the same chick. Talk about a double agent. The girl confessed to both of us, and that was my breaking point. All that drama that led to my divorce is why I want to be single right now.

Chapter 6

Journey

When I knocked on his door yesterday, I was so freaking scared. All I kept thinking was . . .

What if he doesn't like me?

What if he's an asshole?

What if he is just doing it out of pity?

But I was so relieved. He was cool as ice. My fears have all subsided. To have all that he has, he was humble as fuck to be living in a penthouse. I mean, like a really nice dude. So handsome too. I could see Natalia's hot ass flirting with him, so I had to check her after we left. When we walked to the car, I said, "Ummm, what was that all about?"

Her heels were clickety-clacking down the street.

She laughed. "All what?" She giggled innocently.

I mocked her with a girly voice and batted my eyes. "Oh, Mr. Carter, can I pleeeease work for you? Please, I'll suck yo' dick."

"Wait—what? Helloooo—*you* suggested it," we laughed. "I'm sorry, but your dad is fine as hell." She looked around and said in a whisper, "Keep playing, and I *will* suck his dick." I slapped her shoulder, and we laughed. "He should have a warning sign on his door. I was not ready for all of that pretty, caramel-brown skin. And he is soooo tall, looking like fucking Aladdin and shit. It's like your skin on a man."

"He *is* handsome." I smiled proudly.

"Y'all do look related. And the great-grandma, man, you look like her. And you saw Ty. He was a bit flirty. Don't put that shit on me. Keep playing, and you might be my little stepdaughter, so act right." We fell out laughing.

"Yeah, yeah, please just don't embarrass me if he does hire you. I don't want him to think I'm hot in the pants like you."

"Shit, I'm grown, and I've been celibate for months. Yoooou got a lot of nerve, the Queen Ho of Yogaville herself." Natalia did an exaggerated curtsy. "Your body count is way higher than mine. I *was* married."

"Whatever. You're the one on dating sites penis shopping."

"And it's just window shopping. I haven't got one penis yet," she yelled. Natalia pointed to her crotch. "I have nothing but cobwebs down here."

Her alarm beeped, and we got into Natalia's BMW.

"Shut up. I only fucked one Yoga teacher," I snickered.

Natalia spoke into an imaginary mic. "That's her story, and she's sticking to it." She started up the car.

"Okaaaay, and one classmate from Yoga training. He ate my cootch, and I just gave in. We only did it twice. Does that even count?"

"See? Ho ho ho." Natalia pointed to the street as she made a quick turn out of his gated community.

"Hey, I thought a little soak in apple cider vinegar brings my body count down."

"You gonna need a little more than an apple cider, girl. Maybe some holy water." We couldn't stop laughing.

"Sex with a Yogi is awesome, and both of them were so worth it."

"Yeah, so worth it that you had to leave that studio?"

"I know, right?" I gushed, remembering the pressure.

"At this point in my life, I don't need somebody's son jacking up my PH balance. So, I will live my sexual escapades vicariously through you. You had Negroes wanting to do handstand battles for your love."

"You stoooopid. But they *were* competitive. I left because they were paying me pennies to run their front desk and do their online marketing. I was damn near managing the studio. I needed to get a director's salary. Besides, I think Rasshan got back with his wife, and I think Pablo might be bi. I'm good on that. He can keep *that* penis." She turned on Peachtree Street.

"I just think it's so gangsta that your mom would pick an Afro-Cuban brother for your dad."

"Yeah, I think that was her way of sticking it to the family who is so color-struck. It made my life a living hell when I used to visit Colombia, though. The black sheep of the family. The Negrita."

"Well, I guess you are just like your mom since you love them chocolate brothers."

"That I do. No lies detected."

Natalia and I were like two peas in a pod. We met two years ago at Yoga, but it feels like we've been friends forever. I was her instructor during my training, and we'd talk a lot after class. We had a lot in common, so we hit it off. She was going through a rough time and just got out of a very abusive relationship. Before I knew it, I offered her a place to crash for a couple of months until she got her money up to put a deposit on her new apartment.

The healer in me couldn't help it. I've taught Yoga at women's shelters and homeless shelters, and that is not where I wanted her to end up. Even though I still live with my mom, we have a big house in Buckhead, and I offered her the extra bed in the basement, which was the size of an apartment. I never let people get too close to me, but we shared a unique bond. I always attracted friends older than me. My mom has said I had an old soul. I just vibe with people who are more in touch with themselves and want to improve. Girls my age are just hanging at the mall, messing with fuck boys, and watching bullshit reality TV all day.

Natalia and I talk about everything . . . from relationships, self-love, health, spirituality, intuition, spirit guides, shamanic rituals, aliens, other dimensions, and more. She is one of the only friends that know about my gifts, well, some of them. Some things are still better left unsaid. Natalia knows me pretty well aside from my online crew—The Fantastic Four—just not what Janet taught me. She does know I am very psychic.

Natalia's only issue is that she has a really blocked throat chakra and tends to be shy and never really owns her power. She doesn't speak up about how she feels. I think she loves that I have no filter, and I say what she thinks. I gotta say, I think she balances me out with her poise and class since I know I can be a bit abrasive at times with my opinions. I always wanted a big sister, and I'm thrilled that she is mine. I love that even though she is older, I can teach her things as well.

***

After she dropped me off, I finally called back Phil, who was blowing my phone up all day.

I walked in big strides around my room. Then I played with a crystal on my windowsill and admired the garden. My voice was low and stern. "Hello, Philip Anthony Esposito."

"Oh, you're saying my full name. You mad at me?"

I cleared my throat. "Well, I didn't see my monthly deposit in my Cash App. I thought we had an agreement on how this was gonna go?"

"Come on, Journey. It's Sunday. I'll get you tomorrow. You got something for me tomorrow?"

"Yeah, yeah, I got you. See you tomorrow at the studio."

Phil and I helped each other out. He was a friend I met at Yoga through his wife, who was a student of mine. He was just one of many with whom I had "special arrangements." I have to hide most of the money and gifts I receive. My mom already thought I was doing something illegal, like a scam or something. But I never really needed to go that far. I'm a woman who specializes in making people feel special. My gifts help empower people and make them feel good about themselves. And I have to say, these talents haven't let me down yet, and the more I practice on these people, the better I get.

I've had the longest "arrangement" with Phil for over a year now. He had a bad car accident, and his wife got him some private lessons with me to help him get back in shape. It didn't take much. He's a handsome, silver-haired, pretty fit 56-year-old Italian man. He's balding in the middle, but you can tell he was good looking back in the day. I knew he was attracted to me from day one, but I just kept it professional. He's too old anyway. When his gift cards ran out, he secured me for another three months, which was a blessing since I had some credit cards to pay off.

It all started in one private class over a year ago. I was holding him in a handstand. His bulge was so hard that it was embarrassing. He doesn't wear underwear either, so I tried not to look, but I couldn't resist. He was packing an Italian sausage up in them shorts. When he came out of it, he was beet red from embarrassment.

"I'm sorry. I mean, Journey," he whispered, "you are so sexy. I can't take it anymore. I just need one night. I know you feel it . . . the heat between us. Can you?"

"I think you are very attractive, but you're married, Phil. I don't do that."

"Okay. I'll respect that," he mumbled. "For now."

After that, I knew I had him where I wanted him, and I would make sure I smelled delicious and looked sexy every damn time. I wore leggings and bra tops that truly accentuated my shape. I would put him in positions and lean on him closer than needed. I was flirting even more since we booked later appointments in the studio when no one was around. He was a lawyer and got off late. I figured I'd get him to tip me big but had no idea I could really get him to pay a serious bill. So I did a little more to entice him each session to turn up the heat, and it was so much fun seducing him.

I told him I would give him some one day, but I had to work my way up to it. I played that I was nervous and on the fence. Some sessions, I didn't even go through with the full Yoga lesson. I would just sit across from him with my legs crossed and take him through meditation. Like one time after the meditation, we just breathed deeply together. I said in my mind, It's getting so hard. So hard. You are going to come. You are so close to my pussy. *Then out loud, I whispered, "Soon, I'ma let you touch it, papi. I promise." Then* bam . . . *Just like that, Phil jizzed right on himself like a pathetic 14-year-old boy.*

"I'm so sorry. I gotta change . . . Fuck. Fuck . . . I gotta change."

I threw a towel on him and laughed.

"Journey, what's the matta with you? You get a kick outta torturing me? I thought . . . I thought

we were friends, you and I?" He smirked, covering his wet spot with the towel.

"Yes, but you don't get rock hard for your friends. I see how you look at me. I won't tell on you, though. I know Mrs. Esposito would not be pleased if she knew what happened today."

"Oh, come on. Please, don't tell her. She wouldn't let me hear the end of it. She'd kill me."

"I knoooow she is not fucking you. It's understandable." I stood up over him and let him get a good look at my body. "You're a man who has needs."

"Yes," he said in a low voice and sat up, still on the floor. He was at eye level with my crotch. "Yes, and I know you have needs too."

"Phil, I'm not going there with you. I said I might, but not now."

"Okay, but what if we could have an arrangement to get you there?" He raised his hands. "No sex. You could just keep teaching me weekly, say two times a week. And maybe at the end, do what you just did but talk to me in Spanish. It's soooo sexy, Journey. I don't know how you are not taken yet. If I were twenty years younger, booooy, I would have married you in a heartbeat. Let's do this—How does $400 every Monday sound to you."

"On top of your class fee? $500 every Monday. I have a lot of bills, Phil."

He tilted his head. "So, you gonna make it worth my while?"

"You just want to cum, right? With no sex?"

"Well . . . You know I'd rather have sex, but just you, your voice, turns me on. You just got this drippy sexy thing about you. Shit, Journey. Okay, $500."

"I like your plan. I can think of some things to make it fun while you learn." I winked and walked over to the locker rooms slowly so he could get a good look at my bright pink leggings.

Just recently, I said to him, "I think what we do now is still healthy and healing. I hope when you go home, you at least fuck the shit out of Helen."

Phil scoffed at me. "Are you kidding me? She *definitely* gets it good when I get home. She thinks it's just Yoga. Ya know, it's improving my vitality and blood flow. She wants me to keep coming to you. Helen has no idea it's really you and that sweet, young body you have that keeps me going." His hand softly cupped my ass. I gently pulled his hand away. "Now, Philip, what are the rules?"

"No touching. I'm sorry. Fuck. I'm throbbing over here."

I had him right where I wanted him. He was a consistent client who would be one of my investors regardless of whether he knew it.

***

A lot of my extra side hustles I kept on the low-low. Phil was just the beginning, and then I added Michael, Adrian, Ellis, and Alonzo to the mix. I use private Yoga classes and VIP Yoga skills workshops as my cover since my mother has been watching my spending lately. She's so nosy, asking me where I got certain things. I also have a separate account just for their money that goes into my savings. I don't have sex with these guys . . . well, not all of them. It's just fun to tease them. I was glad there were no cameras inside the studio, or I would have been fired by now.

I don't tell Natalia too much about my arrangements even though I trust her with my life. I knew she would totally judge me. I tell her what she needs to know. I need her in my corner. She was so helpful in supporting me when I finally decided to search for Ty. All my life, I had a gaping hole in my heart for not having a connection with my real dad. I was depressed for years and never really understood why. It's like my spirit felt I was living a lie. The confirmation of knowing I was lied to for twenty-two years put a strain on my relationship with my mom. I always knew there was more to the story, but the more in tune I became from meditation and doing my daily Yoga practice, the more I saw an immense shift in me. I knew I had something special. I'm really good at getting what I want.

In school, I excelled because I was excellent at guessing the answer to things I didn't even study. I was even accused of cheating at times because I had identical answers to someone sitting behind me who was pretty smart. I realized then I might not just be a good guesser. I was able to "see" the answer in my head. Almost like I was floating over them and spying. I tried it several times and closed my eyes, and each time, it worked. When I couldn't guess, I would just take a deep breath, and the answer would come. That's actually what led me to study intuition.

The famous, world-renowned psychic, Edgar Cayce, would sleep with a book by his head and wake up knowing all its contents. That shit blew my mind. I figured maybe that was what I was doing. After that, I learned about Robert Monroe, who taught about out-of-body experiences, and I knew then that was something I was doing at will without even realizing it. I'm a force to be reckoned with at only 22, and I am just getting started.

Chapter 7

Ty

Even though I had nothing to hide, I was glad Jocelyn's shift was ending. Today was Natalia's first day interning for me. We agreed on her coming three nights a week after her day job. I could see Jocelyn being a bit nosy, trying to get to know her, so it's best this way. I didn't need any distractions.

I wanted to see what knowledge she had about the industry and maybe even learn more about who Journey was too. Natalia came in looking very professional. Her hair was in a high bun, and she wore a beautiful blue wrap dress that accentuated her curves but still left something to the imagination. She was even finer than I remembered.

"Hey, Mr. Carter."

"Natalia, so good to see you again."

I led her to the office, and we sat down by my desk. "Before we get started, I wanted to give you a little background on the company. The C&C Investment Group works with a team of realtors and independent investors to choose buildings that we want to buy. You know that big building near Ponce City Market? That's one of our current projects."

"Wow. Really? That's a great location."

"Yes, as they say, location is everything. That leads me to your first assignment." I waved to her to move closer and look at the map on my computer screen. "I want you to research this area in detail. It's a ten-mile radius. You'll use the real estate database that we have access to. I'll email you the password."

"Okay, but that looks like the real rough side of town. Are you doing a lot of flipping?"

"It depends. Sometimes we just want the block, and we'll gut it out and start fresh. In many cases, it's cheaper and safer to start over than to do patchwork on a building. We're focusing on rentals right now, so only look for residential buildings."

"How many locations do you want me to find?"

"Impress me," I winked. "You have until Friday. I want you to take a look at how vacant they are, how many people are currently living there, how much repair is needed, and if you can go check the places out and take photos, that's even better. The site I'm going to send you will have that info."

Natalia was typing up notes fast on her laptop. "Sure, I can do that. Maybe on my lunch breaks, I can check out some spots."

"I like your enthusiasm. That's great. Having a hustle will help you go far. Just know that most of the job can be done from home and on weekends, but for the first month, until we get into a little groove, I'd still like you here three days a week. I want to train you so that you will feel comfortable on your own. I always need extra hands on deck since we're acquiring more properties with the market being down."

"Definitely. I would love to be involved in it all. I will only do Uber on weekends, so I have more time for your projects."

"It's technically a project management job that I want to train you for, but I still need admin help. We also need some help with our social media. We get a lot of DMs and need someone to check them more regularly. Once you know what you're doing, I'll put you on the payroll, and I doubt you'll need to do Uber anymore." I raised my eyebrows.

"I am soooo grateful, Mr. Carter. Thank you for believing in me."

"Oh, no worries. I gotta give you a shot, being Journey's friend and all. How is she doing anyhow?"

"Oh, please, she's been over the moon since she met you. You have no idea. She can't stop talking about you. I'm glad you were so open to receive her. She's been through a lot with her mom and knowing you're around just helped her so much. You were the missing link."

"I'm glad. She made me remember why I donated my sperm, to begin with. It feels good to know I helped make a beautiful child and wonderful young lady."

"Yes, she's a special person. She's been a blessing to my life."

"Do you mind me asking how you two became so close since you're so much older?"

"I knew her from Yoga. It's like a little family. I was going through a pretty rough breakup, and my ex-husband wouldn't leave the apartment after we ended things. I had six more months left on the lease, and I refused to deal with any more of his verbal and emotional abuse. Journey was kind enough to open her doors to me to stay with her and her mother."

"Wow, that was nice of them. Sorry you had to go through that. So, is he out of the picture?"

"Yes, Lord, yes. Restraining order and all. I haven't seen him since the divorce."

"Well, I'm glad you closed that chapter. I know how divorce can be."

She smiled nervously and put her head down.

I said, "I'm sorry. I hope I didn't stir up any bad memories."

Natalia shook her head, "Oh no, not at all. I'm actually happy to be free and single." She crossed her legs.

"Me too." I smiled and glanced at her legs. I need to stop doing that.

She tilted her head at me.

I corrected myself. "Oh, I mean, me too. My divorce was petty and nasty. Didn't mean that I'm happy you're single," I chuckled. "Wow, that was awkward."

"It's okay, Mr. Carter. I got what you meant." She smiled.

"Natalia, since we're going to be working together on this project, why don't you call me Ty?"

Natalia sat at the desk across from me, researching on her laptop. Her hair was pinned up—really showing off her beautiful cheekbones, eyes, and neck. It was hard not to stare at her, but I remained focused and professional as much as possible. I didn't want to be known as the creepy dad.

"I have a question, Ty, and I don't mean to be disrespectful in any way."

I opened my arms. "Okay, sure. Ask away."

"When you buy these buildings, what happens to the Black and brown people who need to move because the rent increases or you knock down their buildings?"

"Well, that's a good question. It's not always easy, but many times, we buy them out if they are the owners, or if they rent, we suggest some affordable housing and other units that we own that are nearby. We also have partners who own other apartment buildings as well, so they're not left homeless. There are always other options. We give them enough time to move, usually a year. In many cases, we improve their living. I know it might sound harsh, but it's business. Many other investors don't do nearly as much to help relocate the tenants and find them new locations. We also get kickbacks from our partners when we refer new tenants, so we make money that way too."

"Oh, okay." She continued looking at her laptop. Natalia didn't seem too convinced, and I hated the way her energy shifted. I felt like I probably came off as cold and greedy.

"Don't worry. You're not working for a slumlord. We do a lot of good work in the community too," I smiled.

"I know you do. I was just curious about how it all worked. I found this article from a few years ago saying your net worth was $3.5 million and how you bought up all the properties in East Point in Atlanta. Honestly, it didn't put you in the best light. They kind of painted you as an aggressive shark who just takes whatever he wants, so it sparked my curiosity."

I peeked over her shoulder. "Oh, the *Atlanta Observer*. Candace Overton wrote that, right?"

"Yeah. How did you know? You remember that article from a few years ago?"

"Oh, I remember. She and I used to date, and she's still a little salty is all. Those numbers are old now as well and not accurate at all. The company is worth more than double that."

"Wow, that's impressive, Ty."

"Thanks. She's just using her words to get back at me—petty nonsense. I don't pay her any mind. And regarding the money, it's most likely my assets they're trying to estimate the total of. They don't know my real worth. Nosy folks tried to investigate, but I have things protected as well. Offshore accounts, cryptocurrency, stocks. You know the deal."

"Yes, diversify. That's the way to go."

I got serious and pointed at her. "Look, if I tell you too much, I'll have to kill you."

Natalia raised her hands in surrender. "No, no! Please let me at least finish out this internship. It's only my first daaaay." We started laughing.

"I'm joking, but not bad for your first day, Natalia. I'm seriously considering hiring you. Let's see some more of your findings first, and we can start looking at areas you might fit in best within the company."

"Seriously? Don't play. I'll quit my job tomorrow."

"Yes, let's give it a full month and take it from there. We have new opportunities coming up within property management as well."

Someone knocked on the door. I rose, smiling. "That's just my partner, Marlon Conner, the chief financial officer, the other C in C&C. He's our numbers wiz and is here to meet you."

"Really? Meet me?"

I went to the door to greet him, and Marlon entered and gave me a pound. He was dressed sharp as usual, wearing a gray suit and no tie.

He was so loud. "What's happening, maaaan? You ready for Saturday?"

"Me? Come oooon, you know I stay in the gym, and I'm running six times a week. Your lazy ass just walking around the golf course." We laughed as I slapped him on the back and led him into the office. Natalia stood up, smiling.

"Well, helloooo, Miss Natalia." Marlon said it with a little too much sleaze in his voice. I cringed as he shook her hand.

"Hello, nice to meet you, Mr. Connor."

"Sit, please sit." He sat down next to her. "And noooo, we are not that formal here. Please call me Marlon. We're happy to have you."

"Well, thank you. I'm very honored to work with such a prestigious company as C&C Investment Group. One day, I'd like to learn more about the financial side as well. I hear that is your specialty."

"Sure. What exactly interests you about finances?"

"I'm just curious about mortgages, hard money lending, looking for the right investors. There's a lot I want to learn from you all."

"Well, Natalia, you're in the right place. I'd be happy to take you on a tour of our downtown office and show you some things. Are you coming to our game Saturday? You can meet some more of the team."

"Game?" Natalia looked at me for details.

"Oh no—it's not a big deal." I waved my hand. "Marlon thinks he's Michael Jordan and just wants to show off. We play basketball for a local league."

Marlon stood up. "And we are *crushing* them. We're going to win the championship once again. You so damn humble." He shouted to Natalia, "Boss man over here had twenty-six points last game."

"Wow, that's impressive."

I sat down next to her. "Well, if you're free, you and Journey can come by and see the old man in action. We could use some more cheerleaders."

"Oh, I'm sure Journey would love to see that. I'll see if I can make it."

"It's one p.m. Saturday. I'll text you the details."

"Okay, sounds like fun."

Marlon reached in his pocket. "Natalia, here's my card. Hit me next week if the boss man lets you come, and I'll take you around."

"Oh boy, just don't go giving her none of your work. She is a part-time intern right now. You get your assistant to do your stuff."

"Yeah, yeah. A'ight. I'll see you both on Saturday. I gotta head out for a dinner meeting." He winked at me. "No need to walk me out, Ty. I see y'all got work to do. Nice meeting you." He waved and rushed out to meet with one of his Tinder dates.

"He's a character," Natalia said.

"That's an understatement, but he's been my right-hand man since I started the business and my best friend since college. I know you can't tell, but the brother is a genius with projections and finances overall. I'm good at finding sales and closing deals."

"That's what it takes. The Dynamic Duo. It seems like you have a great synergy together."

"Definitely, Carter and Connor Investment Group started with just us and an idea, and now we clean up brokering major deals. So, let me show you how to get into the site now." She moved her laptop over to me, and I typed in the company password. I showed her how to navigate the system and get started.

I had a few calls to make, so I let her work. She was very focused, and I even heard her make a few calls, doing some research. After three hours of work, she said, "I got a few spots you might like, but I'll put them all in a spreadsheet for you."

"That sounds good. Next week, you can come with me to a construction site and meet some more of the team that might not make it to the game."

She put her laptop back in her bag. "Sounds good to me. I'll get to work on this research."

I was sneaking a peek when she wasn't looking. She was so polished . . . the dress, the shoes, her nails. She definitely would be a great addition to the team. I love having people with class represent me.

I walked her to her car in the parking lot. "Again, I can't thank you enough for this opportunity," she gushed.

She reached out her hand to shake mine.

"Oh, come oooon, you're a part of the family." I opened my arms and hugged her. Her hair smelled like vanilla. Her perfume was light. We hugged a little longer than necessary. It wasn't just me either. We released at the same time, realizing there was chemistry. She avoided eye contact with me as she rushed into her car. I waved and walked back to the building, mumbling to myself, "Yep, I got work for her."

Chapter 8

Journey

I was so happy to get an invite from Ty today. He sent me a text to invite me to his basketball game tomorrow. He wants Natalia and me to come out and support his company's team. He was starting to include me in his life. I wanted to meet his team too since they will eventually be a part of *my* team to help me with A Place for Janet. I couldn't wait to tell Natalia.

I called her on Facetime. "Hey, girl, we just got invited to a basketball game Saturday."

"What's up, Journey? Yes, I know. Ty and Marlon invited us today."

"Oh shoot, I forgot you went to work there today. Who's Marlon?"

"He's his partner and bestie. Nice-looking bald guy too. Very sharp and very chocolate. He is the extra C in C&C Investments. Marlon Conner is his full name."

"I think I remember him when I first started researching Ty. He's more behind the scenes, and Ty is more the face of the company."

I was kind of jealous that she was getting to know Ty even more than me, but I figured having her there would help me in the long run.

"I said I was going to the game, but I might have to leave early. I'll still show my face, though. He wants me to meet more of the team."

"Oh, this is going to be fun, Nat. I wonder if pops can ball."

"Apparently, he can since they won last year's championship. Marlon said he gets good scores. As tall as Ty is, he probably dunked too."

"Against what? Some old fifty- and sixty-year-olds?" I laughed. "Probably a bunch of grandpas."

"Girl, don't sleep. Them older men can play. Ty's only like forty-one or forty-two, so he's not even old yet. Keep talking shit. You gonna be older someday."

I pulled the phone closer to my face to be dramatic. "Wow—so defensive. Let me find out someone has a crush."

"Noooo, stop it, girl. I'm highly impressed with how he moves, how he runs his operation. I mean, it's a tight ship. I don't even think he needed to hire me. He was just doing it to be nice to you. They have a whole office downtown on Peachtree Street. Ty is really rollin' in it. I'm learning so much. I'm guessing he's worth at least ten million by now."

"Get out. Where did you get that number from? I didn't find that anywhere."

"Well, a few years ago, he was worth three-and-a-half million, and he said that he's doubled his assets and then some. He said he has a lot of investments and stuff. The brother is a genius. He's only ten years older than me and making moves that some sixty-year-olds are just now making."

I plopped down on my bed and sighed. "It's pretty surreal. I still can't believe my sperm donor is Daddy Warbucks," I smiled.

"You are so lucky. I want to thank you for pushing me to work with him."

"It's no big deal. I saw an opportunity for you *and* me."

Natalia looked surprised. "Soooo, why don't you do me a favor and find out more about how he does his donations and charities. I eventually want to pitch him my idea officially and get him to be involved. I'm going to need your help in putting it together. You know how to do those fancy decks and stuff."

"Uh-uh. Don't put me in the middle of that. That is *not* my place. *You* should talk to him about that. It's gonna look too suspicious. I'm sure he'll help you. Just give it some time."

"Come on, use your womanly charms." I shimmied my boobs in the camera. "I saw how he was checking you out. Come on. Do it for me, friend.

If you just slip it into the conversation, he would never even know. Get him to say, 'Sure thing, I'll give Journey $200 grand. That's no biggie.'"

"See? One minute, you're teasing me for flirting, and now, you wanna pimp me out for intel."

"That's what friends are for, no?" I smiled innocently and batted my eyelashes.

"It's too soon. I don't want it to look suspicious. He has to trust me. He's already talking about making me a property manager and helping him with his social media pages."

"Word . . . That's pretty dope. You're going to be running shit soon and can teach me."

"I don't know why you didn't just ask to be an intern for him too."

"I didn't want to seem too thirsty."

"Listen, I'm trying my hardest to keep it professional. I should have known you had a hidden agenda. You always plotting." She shook her head.

"Whatever. It's not plotting. It's just planning. I'm a strategic thinker. Play your cards right, and once he starts giving me some money, I'll cut you in."

Suddenly, my mother said, "Once *who* starts giving you *what* money?" She walked up to my cracked bedroom door and pushed it wide open.

"Mom, really? I'm on the phone with Nat."

"Sounds like you're up to no good again." She rolled her eyes at me. I wondered how long she was listening by the door, and I didn't have my earbuds in.

"I was just making a joke. Jeez, can I have some privacy?"

"Whatever, Nini. You are so loud. Close your door then. It is *my* house. Remember that you just *live* here."

"Ooooh, someone's in trouble," Natalia teased.

I shut my door and talked softer. I also turned on the TV to muffle my voice. "Serious, all jokes aside, just butter him up and cater to his ego. Try to find out more about him. I'm so curious to learn more."

"I got you. I was just trying to be strong and behave. He is kinda flirty too, but I see he's trying to keep it professional as well."

"Oh, good. I knew I saw a twinkle in his eye when he met you."

"He's really on top of his game. He might be a little greedy too, just the way he goes after things like a shark. Now, I see where you get it from."

"Oh, fuck you."

"What? That was a compliment–kinda," she laughed.

"Bitch, get off my phone. I'm going to call Kendu now. I haven't seen him in over a week."

"Is your kitty cat missing him?"

"Yes, I seriously need to get some dick."

"Well, go get you some. I'll see you tomorrow. I'll pick you up."

"Okay. Love you."

"Love ya back."

I almost feel like I am a Yogi dominatrix, where I torture men by teasing them, and they pay me for it. Still blows my mind how I can pull it off. I get such a rush from it, though. It gives me so much power. One of my favorite clients is our local celebrity—Adrian Vasquez. He's a pretty famous Puerto Rican comedian from Brooklyn. He was in movies, Broadway, and recently moved to Atlanta to be on a Tyler Perry sitcom. He's sexy and very charming. I love his smile, and he always had me in tears. He reminded me of the kid that always got you in trouble in class for whispering jokes.

His first private session with me started very professionally. He was a bit nervous. He kept shaking his leg on his Yoga mat and biting his bottom lip.

I sat across from him on my mat and lit some incense.

"Soooo, Adrian, what brings you here? What do you want Yoga to do for you?"

"Well, I'm always on the road, working nonstop, so I need something to relax me. You know what I'm saying? I work out and all, but I don't stretch." He smoothed out his shoulder-length waves.

"Why are you nervous?"

"Is it that obvious? I don't know. I guess I'm hoping you don't turn me into a pretzel. I'm so tight." I admired his full beard and sparkling white, made-for-TV teeth. I wasn't into beards, but his seemed so silky and nice.

"Oh, no worries. Yoga is not a competition or about turning into a pretzel. That's such a misconception. I won't go too hard on you. We'll start with some gentle movements."

"Gentle sounds good," he said softly.

"And yes, you men tend to shy away from stretching. Tsk-tsk." I got up and stood behind him. He turned and looked up at me from his mat.

"Just relax. Take a deeeep breath."

I stretched out his arm. He looked at me in shock. "Yo, that felt good. Do the other arm, please."

"I was. I can't leave you uneven now, can I?"

"Eeeeyoooow. Damn, and we're just getting started? Oh, and you smell really good, by the way."

"Thank you. I try."

I walked back in front of him. "That was not Yoga. Just a little bonus."

"Can I be honest with you, Journey? I wanted alone time with you. Shit, that sounded creepy, but I just wanted you to teach me alone, so I wouldn't get embarrassed in class. I figured I could learn better, and I . . . I'm . . . kinda crushing on you. You're like a legend here. Everyone raves about you. At least what I read in the Google reviews and on their website."

"Ah, that's sweet. I think you're adorable, but I'm seeing someone. And I don't date clients."

"Nah, it's cool. It's cool." He shook his head nervously. "That's a lucky dude." He cleared his throat.

"Okay, let's get started, shall we?" I was feeling the sexual tension building between us. Maybe because it's been over a week since I got some, or maybe because he was pretty famous and was sweating me like I was the famous one. I just knew I was gonna enjoy this and milk it for what I could.

I took him through a few slow vinyasas to get his body warmed up. He was somewhat in shape but just had terrible lungs from smoking too much, I bet. He was always doing his standup with a cigar or cigarette in his hand. After only thirty minutes, he was winded. Adrian's chest was heaving up and down like he just ran a marathon.

"That was awesome, Journey." He patted the sweat on his forehead with a towel. "I feel loose. It's like you woke up my body."

"I'm glad you liked your first time. I was easy on you," I winked.

He watched me spray my mat with essential oils and roll it up neatly. He didn't try to hide his gawking.

"So, is there any other bonus with this class?" He wrinkled his forehead.

"Getting me a hundred percent to yourself is the bonus." I stared directly into his eyes.

Adrian rose from his mat to meet my gaze. He folded his mat up sloppily and walked toward me with his towel over his shoulder. "Oh yeah, a hundred percent?" He knew his ass was sexy and was trying me.

"Don't be silly. You know what I mean."

"I don't knoooow. You came highly recommended, and your bonuses are what sold me. One of my boys comes to you."

"Really? Who?"

"Nah, he told me not to tell you."

He stood behind me closely and looked into the mirror. I couldn't lie. He was turning me on by being so aggressive. He was not even my type, really, but I liked his confidence. I'm sure it was Phil who bragged about me. He's an entertainment lawyer and hangs around guys like him. I was just surprised Phil would want to share me.

"So, no extra, extra bonus? Like, can I feel your booty real quick?" he laughed.

I answered with a straight face, "For $100, sure."

"What—so you just selling feels out in these streets?"

"It just went up to $200."

"Nah, for real. You would let me?"

I tilted my head to the side. "You can Cash App me." I raised my eyebrows.

He sucked his teeth. "Only two hundred? I got two hundred. That's chump change. You not fucking with me, are you?"

He went in his wallet and handed me two one hundred-dollar bills. Wow, that was easy. I was just testing him. I took his hand and brought him to the back bathroom. Everyone was already gone for the night, but in case someone happened to pop in, I didn't want to get caught. I don't know what got into me, but I was so horny. I guess I wanted him to go back and tell Philip. I wanted them all to want me even more.

When we entered the bathroom, I pushed him against a wall. Then I stood in front of him and leaned my ass on him. "Go ahead, touch it."

He palmed my cheeks and started rubbing them kinda rough. "Yo, you are wild. I love it." His hands slowly caressed my thighs and ass and then started to ride up my shirt.

"Uh-uh—I said the butt only."

"Damn, you out here giving me à la carte menu?"

"Times up." I turned around.

"Not fair. You didn't tell me I had a time limit."

I was wet between my legs, and my nipples were hard, so I couldn't keep up the serious facade for long. He could see my excitement right through my sports bra.

"So, how much you need for more time?" He tapped my chin and stuck his very hard bulge out so I could see. "See what you did to me? Gyrating and pressing that nice, juicy ass up on me? Damn, you feel good, baby." He grabbed me closer by the waist. His raspy voice was turning me on. He had that New York cockiness that was hard to resist.

"Adrian, that's all you get to touch. I ain't no prostit—" He grabbed my face and started kissing me. Shit. He was kissing so deep, sucking on my lips, my neck, and collarbone. So damn passionate. His hand went in between my legs. "Oh, it's hot down here, girl. Why you fronting?"

"I . . . wasn't. I gotta just keep my cool. You know damn well I shouldn't be doing this." We both smiled. He stroked my pussy and pulled me in closer. Adrian's hands reached for my breasts and caressed them, popping up my top.

"Wait, slow down." He started to suck my nipples. "I-I shouldn't be doing this," I sighed.

He stopped and looked into my eyes with a confident smirk. "But why are you?" He took his long dick right out of his Yoga shorts. It was sa-

luting me like a minibat. He wasn't a big guy, so it took me by surprise.

"Goddamn. You better put that thing away." I couldn't take my eyes off it.

He laughed. "Oh, you not ready for all of this yet?"

"No." I actually wanted to drop to my knees, suck it, and sit on it. But I had to keep him *wanting* me. *I tried to hold out and tease him. I had to keep him contributing to my cause. Finally, I had him where I wanted him.*

He packed his trunk away in his boxers, but I couldn't stop looking at it.

"Can I see you again next week? Can we do that again too? Same deal?"

A cha-ching went off in my head. I'm sure glad I had my mom's shrewdness. "Sure. On top of the private Yoga fee."

"You drive a hard bargain, Yoga Princess. But I think you're worth it." He moved closer to me again, pinned me to the wall, and said in my ear, "Let me just jerk off and look at it. Please? I can't go home like this."

He started to pull my leggings down, and I didn't stop him. I moaned, "Shit. I can't take this. That's going too far." I started to walk away and pull up my leggings, and he pulled me back. Adrian was not letting me say no. He pushed his hardness on me and started sucking my neck and grabbing my breasts. He was rough with me, and I liked it.

"Come on, Journey. If you not gonna gimme some, just let me finish. I can't walk around with this hard dick." He turned me around, yanked down my leggings to my thighs, and took it out to slap it on my ass.

"Damn, Adrian."

He cupped my ass. I pulled my pants down to my ankles. I could not believe we took it that far. A part of me wanted him just to slide in and take advantage of me, but the other part said, hell no. We didn't have any condoms either.

He was in ecstasy. "Oh shit. Yesssss. Keep it just like that."

He started to jerk off, and I said in his head, You will one day get me, so make sure you keep paying me. One day soon, I'm gonna fuck you so good. Not today. You behave—not today.

I shook my ass and made my cheeks wiggle. I made it bounce like a stripper. I did take a few pole dancing classes, so I had some skills. He moaned. "Oh, ooooh my God, Journeeeey. You so fucking nasty. Yeah, bend down to the ground. Just like that." He slapped my ass, and the sting felt so good.

I turned around, dropped to my knees, and cupped his balls. I grabbed his dick. "You're taking too long." I shoved his dick into my mouth, and he screamed like a girl.

"Oh shit, what the fuck? I'm coming. I'm coming." He laughed at himself. He fell against the wall, and I got up smiling. "I'm sorry, love. Damn, I didn't know you were gonna do that. Man, you got a mouth on you." I handed him a paper towel and wiped my mouth.

I was in charge. I felt so powerful. I pulled my leggings back up. I kept a straight face like all of that didn't just go down.

"See you next week?"

"Hell fucking yes. Yo, you dangerous, Journey. Goddamn, you 'bout to make a nigga empty his bank account."

I washed my mouth out and my face while he stood there stunned at what had just happened.

"Get cleaned up. I gotta lock up."

"A'right. Gimme a minute. I can barely stand straight." He laughed at himself.

I walked off with a satisfied grin.

Playing seductress can get me so worked up, but I never ever plan on having sex with my students who pay for "extra services." However, only one person quenches my thirst. That one person is Kendu. He is six feet four, built like a linebacker, and doesn't talk too much. And most of all, he treats me like I'm a goddess. There is a drawback—he's not the sharpest knife in the drawer but was so good at fulfilling my needs. It was pretty pathetic since I could snap my fingers, and he'd come running.

We've been messing around for about six months now, but lately, I've been so busy working that I haven't heard from him as often as I used to. I guess he got annoyed with me for taking too long to call him back. I called today, and he just sent me to voicemail more than once. I saw on his IG story that he was out and about, so I know he was ignoring me on purpose.

I put down my phone and said softly, "Wow, that's not like him."

I went over to my prayer altar and lit a little white candle and some incense. It helps get me into the mood to meditate. I've been reading up on out-of-body experiences, so I thought I'd try out a new technique I just learned. I've done it before without trying or knowing what I was doing, so this time, I wanted to see if I could do it on demand. I lay on my Yoga mat and started to do some deep breathing. It took me a good fifteen minutes to get into a state of deep relaxation. I pictured myself in front of Kendu's house. I saw his door clear as day, even down to the chipped gray paint. I heard music playing and went inside. It was as if I had just walked through his door. I was floating, not really touching the ground. I heard a girl laughing in the back room. I was instantly in that room hovering over them.

I couldn't believe the girl was Zuri. She was this cute Indian girl I knew from Yoga. A brown-skinned chick with long hair fit for a shampoo commercial and nails that look like claws. I'm sure he was into her big fake ass. That's what got her all the attention. Kendu always claimed he hated fake bitches and loved that I was so natural with no work done, and I kept my nails natural. Yet he was all over her, kissing her and tickling her. I jumped from the vision and hoped that was just me imagining that. "That motherfucker."

It looked so real. Could I even imagine all that? I grabbed my car keys.

"Fuck it," I mumbled. As I walked down the hall, I shouted toward my mom's office, "Mom, I'll be right back. Do you need anything from the store?"

"Yes, Nini. Can you get me some almond milk and paper towels?"

"Okaaaay." I rushed out and jumped into my Benz. "Let's see if I'm making up this shit."

I drove so fast to his apartment, and wouldn't you know it . . . Right in front was her fucking red Infiniti. "This bitch."

I parked and called him again.

"Hey, Journey, what's up, mami?"

"You tell me. Open the door, Kenduuu." I walked up the stairs.

"What? What? You're here? You doing surprise pop-ups now? What's that about?"

"Just open the door, Kendu. I wanna see you." I started knocking incessantly.

"Chill, chill. Why you tripping? I'm in the back."

"Are you coming?"

"Damn, I-I'm in the middle of something right now."

"Oh really? What's her name?"

"Just promise to relax, Journey. I'm coming. It's not what you think, so relax." He slowly opened the door. We both hung up our cells. He looked so damn good with a gray tank top, fresh haircut, and his biceps were popping. I hated him for being so fine.

"Relax?" I folded my arms and tried to peek over his shoulder down the hall.

"Yeah, relax. You know how you blow things outta proportion. I'm working on a photography project for someone you know. You know Zuri, right, from Yoga?" He cracked the door open more, and when I stepped in, he stunk of perfume when he hugged me.

"Photography project? Riiiight. Of course, I know who Zuri is." I sucked my teeth and folded my arms. "And so you had to keep sending me to voicemail?"

"Yes. I was working, babe." He turned his head and shouted, "Zuri, can you come here, please?"

She came prancing out of his bedroom in a hot pink bikini with a crochet cover-up.

"Oh, oh, hey, girl." She looked afraid and like she was trying to play it off.

I looked her up and down. "Oh, please, don't 'hey, girl' me. So, what the fuck is going on?"

"Whaaaat? Who you talkin' to like that, Journey?" She had one hand on her hip.

"You . . . Nah, I'm talking to both of y'all. This shit looks real suspect." I turned to Kendu, who looked like he was kinda enjoying it. "Why are you smirking? You know what? I'm good. Enjoy your photo session . . . It's not even worth the drama."

He grabbed my shoulder, and I looked down at his grip. He slowly released it.

Zuri's voice was so high-pitched and whiny. "We wasn't even doing nothin'. Stop bugging out for no reason. He's taking photos of me for my Instagram. I'm building my marketing platform to sell bikinis and beachwear."

"It's cool. Good luck with that. I'm out," I said.

Kendu followed me downstairs to my car. "Journey . . . Journey. Stop overreacting. Just chill. We're almost done. I-I didn't tell you since I knew you would react exactly like this."

"Whatever. You just got busted. I'm done. I got to run to the store for my mom." I looked up and saw Zuri was standing in the doorway, taking it to another level after I was down the stairs.

She screamed, "Journey, don't nobody want your man. We just became friends in Yoga, and he told me he was a photographer. Stop making it something it ain't. You always think the world revolves around you."

I wanted to drop-kick and drag her by her long hair so bad. I stared at her with so much hate. "He's not my man. He's all yours. Stop making a scene. It's not very ladylike of you. Have some class. Ooops, I forgot. You don't have any. Enjoy your photoshoot, boo. Run along." I flung my hand as if I were shooing a fly away. That set her off, and she came running down the stairs yelling some more.

"I'm not making a scene. You coming here on some possessive shit, and from what I know, you two aren't even exclusive. So what if I wanted to fuck him? His dick ain't got your name on it."

I clenched my jaws and almost raised a fist. Kendu held my hands down.

"Keep on with that mouth, Zuri, and I got something to shut it up," I shouted.

Kendu tried to hug me, but I shrugged him off. "Chill, chill. We ain't do nothing at all. I promise."

I smelled her perfume on him, and it made me lose it. "Get off of me. I said I'm out." Tears rolled down my cheeks. I wiped them quickly. I refused to give them the satisfaction.

I wished she would trip and bust her ass on the stairs. I shot her a look and just pictured her falling and hurting herself. What happened was even funnier.

Kendu screamed, "Yo, you closed the door? I don't have my key, and it locks on its own. What the hell is wrong with you, Zuri?" She was in her bikini, freezing her big ass off. It was chilly that night at forty-five degrees.

"Wow, looks like you're going to need a locksmith," I said as I slowly walked to my car. I wanted to hear them arguing. It was hysterical. I laughed so hard when I got in and pulled off.

"Journey, Journey, lemme use your phone. Come on, lemme borrow your phone to call my landlord. Damn. I know you hear me. Fuck."

I just kept walking and got into my car like I didn't hear him. I couldn't wipe the grin off my face. Good for them. They fucked with the wrong one. People get a little twisted when they know I teach Yoga and meditation, but I am truly not the one to mess with. I am not always "peace and love."

Group Video Chat with Fantastic Four

"So, do you remember that dude I was seeing?"

"Kendell or Kendu?" Robbie said, scratching his head.

"Yes, I busted him doing OBE."

Elizabeth gasped. "Get out. It really worked? Like in real time?"

"Yeeees, girl. Something didn't feel right. I saw it in real time, not a dream at all. He just kept dodging my calls, and he never did that. So, I just meditated and . . . *boom* . . . I was at his front door, and I saw the girl was there, and I knew the bitch from Yoga. I drove right over there, and wouldn't you know . . . She was there."

"Say, word," Robbie sat up. "Yo, he's a dick."

"Can you read him for me? I want to know if he ever cared about me and if he feels remorse."

Elizabeth said, "Sure. Text me his info, and I'll have it done by tomorrow morning."

Robbie sounded groggy and said, "Look, I'll try, but I'm not making any promises. I'm still not that good."

"That's why we practice," I said. "And, please, Robbie, you are like the most connected."

Robbie's voice got strong. "But hold up. Why don't we turn the tables? Why you want us to waste our powers on that nigga who already shown you he ain't shit? What's the point?"

Elizabeth tilted her head and shrugged, agreeing. "I mean, he's right, but I wouldn't mind you check in on Professor Dalton to see if he's going to pass me in psychology. He's been on my case."

Robbie's eyes were closed. He took a deep breath. "Does Kendu have a weird birthmark on his cheek or something? It's not big but looks like a little ink blot." He laughed.

"Get out. Yes, he does. What the fuck, Robbie? You are damn good. How'd you get him so good without meditation?"

"I just saw it. Yes, he's a dog. He's sleeping with that girl. Dude got a stable. Might be like three or more."

"What?"

His eyes were closed. "Yes, I'm just getting the feeling, and I even feel it in my stomach that he's lying. So basically, God saved you from a serial cheater."

"You so stupid. But I still want y'all to read him for me. And to be fair, everyone send me one question, and when we meet tomorrow, I'll answer them. Deal?"

"Bet. But you always seem to get what you want, big sis. I see you." He pointed into the screen, and we all laughed.

"Yes, and I love it." I twirled my curls.

"I'm learning a lot from you. Make sure you let Zack know. He had to work at his dad's dispensary tonight." Elizabeth tilted her glasses sarcastically.

"We will learn a lot from each other. I love my fam. I gotta go, though. Chat with y'all tomorrow, gang. I'll text Zack too."

"Peace." Robbie hung up.

Elizabeth waved, "Bye!"

I really love my crew. I might tell them about Ty soon. I'm just not ready for that reaction yet. Not sure how they will take it.

Chapter 9

Ty

The game was exhilarating. The gymnasium was packed and full of excitement. I had even more energy knowing Journey and Natalia were watching me do my thing. Journey was not hard to miss in a bright pink Yoga outfit with a top that said, *Namaste* in big letters. She stood out in the crowd of wives and children, and I have to admit, I was pretty proud of that. Natalia was wearing a hoodie and some tight jeans. It made her look ten years younger, like a college kid. It was definitely a switch from her corporate attire.

I finally made it over to the bleachers after everyone finished high-fiving me for slamming thirty-two points.

"All right, Kobe. I see you," Natalia said and high-fived me.

"Yeah, Ty, I'm so impressed. You still got it, pops." She mumbled "*pops*" and covered her mouth, realizing we were in public. Good thing since I wasn't prepared to tell everyone yet.

Marlon was talking with the coach and then he saw the girls, he came right over with long, confident strides. "Well well well . . . How are we doing today, ladies?" he said with a smile. "Nice to see you again, Natalia, and you must be *the famous Journey.*"

Journey smiled and gave him a flirtatious head tilt. "Yes, that's me." She sized up Marlon with her eyes. Then she reached her hand out to shake his, and he just held on to it.

I cleared my throat to shift the energy. "Yes, Journey, this is Marlon. He is one of my best friends. If things were different, he would have been your godfather."

"Get out."

Marlon said, "Yeah, but, of course, it's too late for that. So, did you ladies enjoy seeing them firefighters get their asses beat? One more game, and we'll be Fulton County's finest."

"Do you get a ring or something?" Journey teased.

"Nah, just a shout-out on the Facebook page and a plaque in the gym."

We all laughed.

Natalia said, "I have to say that I was impressed. That was an excellent game."

She glanced at my legs and smiled. Yep, I see she wants it, and she will definitely get it.

I said to Marlon, "So, how about we get cleaned up and have lunch?"

"Nah, man. Remember, I have a closing at four today? I need to be there."

"You don't. That's what our team is for, but okaaaay." I shrugged since it was a lost cause. Marlon was a bit of a control freak.

He said, "Let me do what I do so we can keep the money flowing."

I shook my head and turned to the girls. "Ladies? Lunch?"

Natalia said, "Oh no, sorry. I have to work. Why don't you and Journey go? I saw that banging Thai spot around the corner. I get a lot of Uber Eats deliveries from there. I hear it's delicious. Simi Yum Yums is the name."

"Oh yeah, I heard about it too. I'm down," Journey said.

"Okay. Give me fifteen minutes to get changed."

Marlon said his goodbyes, giving the girls light hugs. Only this time, he took Journey's hand and kissed it. "Journey, it was a pleasure. Here's my card." I raised my eyebrows as he slid her his business card. He turned to me and said, "Man, she really looks like your family. I see it. Genes are crazy."

"Well, what can I say? My genes are strong. She's beautiful." I smiled at Journey and put my hand on her shoulder. I'm gonna have to check him later to stop flirting with young girls.

She blushed. “Ah, you’re too kind. Thank you.”

Simi Yum Yums was a semicrowded restaurant but not too loud. We were a little nervous, but I figured it was expected since this was only our second meeting, and now we were alone.

After we ordered, I figured it would be good to know a bit more about her.

“So, tell me . . . What do you like to do other than Yoga? What are some of your hobbies?”

“I have a lot. Yoga started as one, and then I was so obsessed with the results in my life, so I went and got certified. I love to travel. Interior design is my major and dance. I’m pretty good.”

“Oh yeah? Well, I have two left feet, but I can carry my own in salsa, but definitely, I’m not a pro.”

“Oh, fun. I can teach you. Mom is a great salsa dancer. I spent summers in Colombia too, so we partied. But now, even though teaching is my main source of income, it still doesn’t feel like work.”

“Well, you know what they say . . . You have found success when you can’t tell the difference between work or play.”

“Oh, this is just the beginning. I feel like I’ll consider myself truly successful when I can open up my lifestyle center.”

I leaned in. “Tell me more about that. How and when do you plan on doing that?”

"Ty, I have it all planned out. It's gonna be like those salon suites where people can rent rooms and share common areas. But the focus will be on mind, body, and spiritual businesses—a true wellness center. I'll learn more about real estate first from Natalia, and, of course, you now. I know location is everything."

"This is true. So far, it sounds great. You don't see many places like that in Atlanta. I'll help you where I can. Just get clear on your business plan and know who your audience is, and then I can help point you to the best location."

"You'll help me for real?" Her voice went up an octave like a little girl.

"Sure, but you have a ways to go. Do you have a location in mind that you want to look into?"

"Not sure yet, but I want to own the whole building. I can lease to own if I have to."

"Word? That's ambitious. So, did your mom create a trust fund for you or something?" I teased.

"Nooo, I wish. Nothing like that. I have some investor friends of mine, and Mom will be one of them, I'm sure."

"Okay, so what are you going to give them?"

"Excuse me?"

"You know . . . equity in your company, shares? Haven't you thought that through? What cut are you willing to split with? People won't just give a check without an ROI." She looked flustered and started to sip her water as her brain searched for answers. It seems I struck a nerve. I just saw a flash of an older man giving her money. I guess I was seeing the vision of her clients who were going to help. "You don't have any old men promising you money, do you?" I took a sip of my soda and watched her reaction.

Journey jerked back and rolled her eyes. "Oh God, oh noooo."

She was lying, I could tell.

"What made you ask that?" She held a wide-eyed look.

"Oh, just teasing you. It's Atlanta. Home of the sugar babies."

"That's funny. I have wealthy clients, but it's a mix of men and women."

"Well, when you make a business plan, let me take a look at it. If not, maybe you should start working on that next. I have some folks in my network who might want to help you out." I didn't want to volunteer too much. I wanted her to work hard on her plan and not enable her. But if it were good enough, I wouldn't mind investing. That's why I'm successful. I earned it all. My parents didn't spoon-feed me anything. I have a feeling her mother spoiled her so much she expected a hand-out. Journey's phone kept vibrating on the table.

I pointed to her phone facedown. "Why don't you get it? It's okay. I don't think you're being rude."

She looked at it and slammed it back down. "Nope. It's just some big liar I used to deal with."

"Oh, so you're making him sweat a little bit?" I snickered.

"Nope. I am officially done with this one. He's about to be blocked."

"What did he do?" I was curious about what drama she had going on in her world.

She raised her voice. "Lied to my face and messed around with this thot who claimed to be a friend." She tossed her hair and looked at the couple across from us who were staring. They probably thought she was mad at me.

"Lower your voice." I smiled.

She leaned in closer. "My bad. So tell me something, Ty—were you a dog growing up?"

"Actually, I was. I'm not proud of it. Many young men go through that stage, unfortunately. I can't lie. I had a lot of opportunities." I shrugged my shoulders.

"Oh, word? That's a nice way of saying you had a lot of girls throwing vaginas at you." We both laughed.

"Journey, your mouth." I shook my head.

"Oh, sorry. Too much?"

"Well, as a kid with raging hormones, it can be hard to say no. In my case, I was a little sheltered in my youth and was a late bloomer with the girls. I made up for lost time, though. What sucks is I lost a few amazing women by treating them like shit and also putting my career before them."

"Like your ex-wife?"

"Are you fishing? You sure are a nosy little girl."

She snickered. "Well, I was just curious. I mean, you are a catch, Ty. A wealthy, good-looking man. I'm surprised she didn't fight for you."

"No, not really. I mean, it's a long and complicated story, and I honestly didn't deserve Ava."

"I get it. Grown folks talk." She rolled her eyes sarcastically. "But do you think you'll get married again?"

"Maybe. But I don't think I'm ready just yet. I'm going to work on myself a bit more. Make sure the guy you end up with cares about their personal growth, since in the long run, it will also reflect how he treats you. Whatever you do, don't rush into a relationship now. Enjoy your twenties."

"Oh, you don't have to tell me. I have a lot of girlfriends and students who are much older than me and believe me, I've heard their horror stories. Many I met via Yoga because they came to destress from toxic relationships and many of them even abusive ones. If it's one thing I learned from them and my mom is I don't need a man to validate me."

"That's my girl. So many women will settle for any man for fear of being alone."

"Exactly. But it won't be me." Journey popped a shrimp into her mouth.

"Just don't give the good guys a hard time either. There are some good ones out there, Journey." I took another sip of my soda.

"I'm not going to wait until I'm thirty-five either before I end up having to buy sperm like my mom."

"Ouch! Low blow."

"What? She didn't hear me say it. I mean, I doubt it will come to that."

"Yes, I'm sure you'll find a good mate in due time."

"Yeah, I know. I thought the good guys were lame and went for the bad boys, and where did that get me? Just lied to. And this guy—his name is Kendu. I mean, no kind of remorse. He tried to act like it was no big deal when I busted them together at his apartment."

"Wow, that's a lot. What did you do—search his phone?"

"Nope, I just felt he was lying, and I went over there."

"Yikes. So, you got some reeeeally good spidey senses, huh?"

"It's just hard to lie to me these days. I've been getting good with my intuition. Remember, Natalia told you I was good at knowing things? I know I got it from you."

I was intrigued. "Yes, I can see that but explain it a bit more."

"It's like I can think of something, and I'm spot-on. I can want someone to do something, and they do it."

"That's crazy that you say that. I think I have the same thing, but I always looked at it as just putting a laser focus on a goal and manifesting it."

"It's probably a superpower you passed on to me, and you didn't even realize it."

"You think we have superpowers?" I raised my brows and leaned in.

She took a deep breath and looked directly into my eyes. "Okay, so if I tell you this, don't think I'm crazy. But, real talk, Ty, I saw it just like a flash. A vision. I was meditating, and it came like a vision. And truth be told, he wasn't even really my man yet, but I was hoping we were working toward that. Just don't lie to me; be honest. When people lie to me, it sends me to a dark place."

"Wait, so let me get this straight. You just meditated and saw him with another girl, and she was really there?" My eyes widened as she nodded her head.

"I used to do it a lot without knowing what was going on, but now, I can control it somewhat. It's more than a vision. It's like I'm transported to a place I want to see. I see it like I'm there. I sometimes even feel like—"

"Like what?"

Her shoulders dropped. "You think I'm crazy, I know. Why are you smiling?" She snickered.

"Actually, not at all. Feels like what? Tell me—and I'll tell you why I'm smiling."

"It feels like I'm not a part of my body. It is a bit scary. I hope I can come back within my body when I do it."

"What do you mean? You think you can get locked out?" I laughed.

"You laugh, but I read some wild stories about it, like people doing it and not being the same again."

"I don't think you should play around with that then. I got to be honest. The reason that I'm smiling is that I realize I'm not the only one. My abuela used to tell me it ran in the family. That I should be careful of who I'm around since people want to be around you more when you have the gift. As if they could take it." I laughed. "She was very superstitious. A little paranoid, to be honest."

"No, she probably just meant people would drain your energy. I even teach my Yoga students how to protect their energy with various meditations and breath-work. Many come to my classes stressed out from others and don't even realize they are walking sponges."

"I've had some crazy experiences like that. Some people I just feel are bad news, so I stay clear. I am not too keen on crowds either. But as for the whole floating out-of-body thing, I've done it, but not intentionally. More of being somewhere without really going. I dreamt about it mainly, and it was usually related to a business deal or something."

Journey leaned in. "Really? Like what?"

"Well, one time, I had a big meeting with a corporation who was interested in selling me some commercial locations. The day before the meeting, I dreamt the CEO ended up in the hospital. I was seeing him as if I were in the room with him, standing over him. He told me not to worry, and his legacy would live on. I woke up feeling strange. Like an hour later, I got a call that he died that morning of kidney failure in the hospital and that he was admitted two days before."

"Holy shit. That's crazy."

"I know. I still get chills when I think about it. What's really crazy is that his son, who was the VP, postponed the meeting until after the funeral, and then the deal went through without a hitch."

"His legacy will live on."

"Exactly."

"Oh, wow, that's amazing. You had a premonition for real, but it sounds more like an out-of-body experience than just a dream." Journey took a bite of her peanut sauce shrimp. She seemed to be enjoying it. "I feel you had a psychic vision, and I feel you passed it on to me, but you can't be afraid of it. It's apparent your skills have helped you this far. You probably just didn't acknowledge it as your intuition."

"Well, I don't talk much about this kind of stuff with anybody since it does sound a little crazy." I sipped my drink.

"Yeah, I know, but in my circles, this is common conversation. You know, Yogis are into the spiritual stuff." She shrugged her shoulders. "I have an idea and don't worry. If you say no, it will be okay. I would love for you to meet my mom. So this way, you can see the other half of this masterpiece your seed created." She fluffed up her hair.

I kinda choked on a piece of chicken and wiped my mouth.

"Is the food good? Are you okay?" she asked.

"It's delicious, Miss Masterpiece," I laughed until I coughed. "The red curry sauce is a bit spicy, though."

"How you got all that island blood, and you can't handle the spice?" She shook her head. "So, what do you say to dinner next week? Mom and I can make a traditional Colombian dinner for you. We won't make it too spicy." She leaned in, smiling. This girl was such a trip.

"You know, I think I can do it. That sounds great. What's her name?"

"Excellent. Let's shoot for Wednesday. Her name is Claudia Salazar. She's a bit tough but really sweet when she gets to know you."

"I appreciate it. Just make sure she's okay with it, all right? I don't want to intrude."

"Are you kidding me? She wants to meet you—and quite frankly, she kept you a secret all these years, so she has no choice," she laughed.

I felt a chill go down my spine as I forced a smile. What Journey wants, Journey gets.

Talking to Journey about our "powers" helped me realize that I was not in this alone, and it was nothing to take lightly. I definitely have abused it without knowing what I was doing, and the guilt has been with me for years. The power of my mind still haunts me to this day, since deep down inside, I wonder if it was me that caused my parents' death.

During their car accident, I was in the backseat, and I never understood how I left the scene with hardly even a scratch, and both of my parents died on impact. They had just picked me up from the airport when I arrived back from grad school. The tension between them in the car was pretty thick. I figured they were just arguing over something as usual.

My mom barely looked at my father and tried to make small talk.

"Tylercito, you look so good. I missed you, baby."

"Thanks, Mom. I missed you too."

My father grunted, "This woman could not stop talking about you, like she think you still a baby."

"Oh, he is my baby. Do you want to eat at your favorite restaurant, Velma's Kitchen? We have to celebrate your 4.0 grades."

"Heck yeah. I'm starving."

My father interrupted us. "Well, how the hell you gonna get there? We not going to no Velma's Kitchen. We got the same island food at home."

Mom grimaced, "No, that is Jamaican food. I made Cuban food tonight, and you know it's his favorite, Carl."

He sucked his teeth. "Come on, Millie, not today. You already pissed me off one time."

My mother took a deep breath, then turned back to me. "We can eat what I cooked instead, but we are going to your favorite restaurant tomorrow, okay? I cooked some ropa vieja. You love that too."

She was definitely trying to keep the peace since normally, she would have demanded we go to Velma's Kitchen. Her eyes seemed so weary, and she reached her hand toward the backseat and patted my knee.

"We don't have no money to go eat out. We can just enjoy what's in the fridge. Millie's Kitchen." Dad grabbed the steering wheel and shifted into

another lane while he laughed at his own corny joke.

My eyes went to my mother's wrists which were swollen and bruised. I caught her hand and started to examine it slowly.

"Mommy—what happened to you?"

She snatched her hand back. "Oh, it's nothing. Just clumsy."

"Oh no. Dad, you promised," I yelled as our eyes met in the rearview mirror. "You promised you wouldn't put your hands on Mom. What's going on with you two?"

"No, noooo, it's not your father. I just had a little accident in the garden."

"Oh really? An accident that looks like somebody was holding your wrist so tight? I can see the fingerprints."

The car suddenly sped up, and my father began yelling, "Who ya tink you're talking to, son? You raising your voice at me? You mussa mad."

"You—I'm talking to you. You keep hitting on Mommy like she's a punching bag. Just 'cause you *can't get your shit together. You're so lucky she didn't call the cops on you because I will."*

"Tyler, stop. Please, stop," my mother cried softly.

"You must want for me ta pull this car off da side of de road and trow you out wit' all your shit. And you're lucky I'm driving, or I would have box you in ya smart mouth right now."

I put my face in between the seats and said, "Oh really?"

He pushed his foot down harder. I guess he thought it would scare me. He was going almost ninety mph. He chuckled. "Oh, so you think you're cute? We spend our good earned money to send you off to university, and you come back with this mouth? Hanging with them spoiled rich kids is going to get you put in the damn box six feet under. You keep on. You not the big man you tink."

"Enough, Carl, enough. Please, slow down. You're scaring me."

I sat back with clenched jaws and looked at him with tears dripping from my eyes. I tried to calm down. My mother kept patting my leg. He turned his music up and started singing to Beres Hammond's greatest reggae hits like it was just a lovely Saturday drive. My mother shook her head at me with pleading eyes. It just made me more furious to see her cowering in fear and him not giving a fuck. I couldn't help but think of what a nightmare it must have been for her since I left. I just knew it was getting better since that's what she would tell me whenever I called. But I should have known. It was all a front.

I hate you. I fucking hate you. I wish you would die. Leave us the hell alone. Die. Die, you fucking evil asshole.

Not a word came out of my mouth, but my eyes said it all. He looked up at me and drove faster to spite me. Another car swerved in front of him, and he changed lanes without signaling. Then we heard a loud bang. My mother screamed, and that was the last memory I had of them. The next thing I knew, I was in an ER on a stretcher. I never told anyone, but I think it was me. The heavy weight stayed with me for years. I guess that's why I held on so close to Papa. I feel it was my fault. I didn't want my mom to die—only him. I learned to be careful what I wished for from that day on.

Chapter 10

Journey

I was very excited. It had only been a week since I saw him after the basketball game, and we were going to hang out again. Ty was taking me on a tour of some of his properties to learn more about what he does. He came right on time to pick me up from the Yoga studio in his shiny black Maserati. I was so proud, but I couldn't even brag and say who he was since I didn't want anyone in my business, but I made them wonder.

Tammy, the busybody of the crew, yelled, "Whooo hooo, girl. That's for yoooou?"

I looked back and smiled. "Yes, a good friend. I'll see you guys tomorrow."

She grunted and smiled. "Uh-huh—just a friend."

If they only knew.

When I got outside, Ty rolled down the window and said, "Your chariot awaits." He got out of the car and opened the door for me like the perfect gentleman. I looked back at the studio's window, and the Yoga teachers were staring with their mouths hanging open.

"Hiiii, Ty." I hugged him, then hopped in. The new car smell took over my senses. "Wow, this is so nice." I rubbed my hand across the burgundy leather seats.

"Ah, thanks. One of my newest babies."

I looked at the studio window and saw them pretending to have a conversation . . . but still staring. "Would you look at them? So damn nosy." He looked at the window and waved to the girls, and we laughed as he sped off. He loved the attention, I could tell.

"They think you're my date and not my dad. I didn't tell them anything, though."

"That's gross," he said in a playful Valley Girl voice.

"I know, right? So, where are we off to exactly?"

"Oh, I was thinking we check out my new building that we just finished, and then we can head to Atlantic Station to grab a bite to eat."

"That sounds good to me." I was overjoyed. I felt like a princess.

His phone rang, and Marlon's name came up on the display in the car.

"Hey, what up, what up?" Marlon yelled.

"Hi, I'm in the car with Journey. Ahem," he sarcastically cleared his throat.

"Oh, oh—so, like keep it clean? Gotcha."

I giggled. "Hey, Marlon."

"Heeeey, Miss Journey. How you doing, girl?"

"Great. We're going on a little tour."

"Oh? That's cool. He's showing you around? One day, I can show you some spots we have too."

Ty chimed in. "So, what's up, Marlon?" Marlon was a bit flirty, and Ty wasn't having it.

"Oh, nah. My bad to intrude on Daddy and Daughter time."

"Stop it. Cut to the chase, man." Ty tilted his head and looked at me. I shrugged.

"I want to find out if you went to the leasing office today for Sweetwaters."

"No, I'm actually headed there now to show Journey."

"Cool. Stop by the office. They have a package for you. It's kind of important."

"All right, no problem. Thanks. Peace."

We pulled into the oval-shaped parking lot, and the building was so beautiful. Two tall waterfalls were framing the silver, futuristic structure.

I gazed up at the trees. "This architecture, my God. It looks like something out of a movie. I love it."

"Thanks. I was blessed to have a former classmate create magic for us. Not sure if you're into architecture, but it's by T. Archer Design. We've done pretty well with the marketing. We haven't even opened yet, and we're already at full capacity. I'm still at eighty percent of the construction being done." Ty walked proudly. He stood so straight and regal.

"My goodness. That's pretty amazing. So, aaaah, do I get a family discount if I want to rent?"

"These are condos—not rentals. They start at 700K, but we have other properties, so when the time comes, we can talk about it."

"Holy shit. Did you say 700K? Why in the hell would someone want to buy an apartment for that much? Just get a damn mansion. That makes more sense to me."

"Well, when you got it, $700,000 is chump change. Many of our new residents are either established entrepreneurs, corporate executives making seven figures, or just trust fund babies with long pockets. They like staying in Midtown. Keep in mind, Journey, we have luxury amenities and conveniences. Even a concierge service that will do pretty much anything you need as far as errands go, so it's well worth it. Let me show you what's really selling them on purchasing with us."

The automatic glass doors opened when we walked into the entrance. An aromatic fragrance of honeysuckle took over my senses. Soft jazz played over the speakers. We walked into the lobby and were greeted by beautiful fish tanks embedded in the walls. I felt like we entered a luxurious aquarium. Tall bamboo plants almost hit the ceiling.

"Journey, close your mouth before a fly gets in it," he chuckled.

"OMG, this is incredible." I looked to my left and saw a poster advertising the gym, the lounge, a miniature golf deck, and the spa that were all located on-site. "Oh, now I see why this place is selling. It's awesome. You don't even have to leave. This is the kind of vibe I want my center to have. It doesn't have to be so luxurious, but I love the vibe of it all."

"See, that's why I wanted you to check it out. Get you some inspiration to build on your vision. It's not going to happen overnight, but it's great to see how properties come together from a distant vision in your mind."

I was feeling so good to know that he cared. Ty wanted me to see that anything is truly possible.

"Take a seat. I got to get some mail from the office. I'll be right back."

"Oh, I'll just get lost in the aquarium. It's so relaxing."

When he walked off, I took a few selfies with the beautiful in-wall aquarium behind me. I was really feeling myself. I wish I could post this and say,

Here with my dad chilling at Sweetwater condos–the building he owns.

#mydaddy
#myoldman
#pops
#mydadisbetterthanyourdad

But, of course, I couldn't. At least not yet. He walked back, looking a little stressed, holding a box that was half-open in his hand. It must have been important for Marlon to tell him to get it.

He saw me taking a selfie. "What? I can't get in one?"

"Sure."

He put his arm around me and took the phone from me since he was much taller. We both looked up at the camera and smiled.

"Is it okay?" he asked.

I looked at it, and we looked so good. "Oh, I love it. We really do look alike. I see it in our smiles. Same dimples. But you look more like an older brother."

"I'll take that. You're too kind. I still think you favor your great-grandmother, Mercedes." He sat next to me. "What do you feel like eating?"

"Can we get takeout? I would love just to sit here. It's so relaxing and beautiful. I don't feel like any crowds right now."

"I'm going to show you the cafe area. It's even nicer."

"Can we do tacos?"

"Sure." He pulled up the Uber Eats app on his phone and passed it to me. "Order what you want."

"Wouldn't it be hysterical if Natalia delivered it?"

"Oh noooo. That's cold. I hope to get her on the team, so she doesn't have to do that for much longer. She's working out pretty good so far. Good call." He high-fived me.

"Really? I'm so glad. She seems happy to be working with you." I punched in my order of fish tacos and passed the phone back to him. A part of me hoped he would walk away for a minute so I could snoop through his phone and see if he's said anything about me, maybe to Marlon, but he wouldn't walk away. I guess he's not that gullible.

"Okay, I'm going to get a taco bowl with all the fixin's. I'm hungry."

"I hear you."

"They said it should be here in twenty minutes." We took the elevator to an upper deck where the cafe and lounge with a view were. We sat at a silver table that looked like a small lunch room, but the view was breathtaking. There were smaller in-wall aquariums here, but they were the shape of starfish, and the colors changed every few minutes. It was almost like a cool nightclub.

"So, Ty, can I ask you a personal question?"

"Shoot." He raised one brow slyly. "I'll see if I want to answer it."

"Why did you want to meet with me after so many years?"

"Well, to be honest, when I first made the donation, I knew that there would be a chance later down the line that whoever became my offspring would want to know their roots, so I didn't mind doing it. Aside from some wild family stories I'll share one day, I think I came from a pretty good upbringing with lots of culture. I'm not ready to be someone's father with my lifestyle and all, but I still don't mind connecting with any of the donor kids. I was shocked to hear from you since no one has contacted me yet."

"Even if it's like fifteen or fifty kids coming at you?"

"Okay, Journey, come on. It's not like that at all. And they wouldn't all come at once. For the record, last I checked, there were only about seven or eight kids so far, but I need to double-check. There is a limit. Getting to know you is a very good start." He rubbed my shoulder. "I see a little bit of me in you and not just the smile."

I gushed. "Really? What part?"

"Well, the ambitious part. The swag."

"Oh shoot, you see it? You see it?" I dusted off my shoulders playfully.

"And that vibrant personality. Just the way you talk to people and know how to win them over in an instant. I know I have that as well." He raised his eyebrows. "And I see that you do have a love for helping people, especially the underdog. You know—with your passion for helping the homeless."

I could feel my face was hot from blushing. I felt so honored that he saw our similarities. "I wish I could be more like you. I'm so happy that we can connect and build. I'm eager to learn as much as I can from you, and you know . . . It's when you have time. I don't want you to feel pressure."

"Come on. It's no pressure at all."

"At the very least, I hope I do get first dibs on things since I was the first kid to reach out." I giggled and then realized that joke might not have gone over well.

"Things like what?" His guard went straight up.

"Oh, you know, in case you want to donate a building to me or something." I forced a laugh to ease his anxiety and let him know I was just joking. His eyes watched me intensely as if he could tell there was some truth to my sarcasm. Was he reading me?

"I'm just kidding, Ty." I slapped his hand. "I will work for what I want to get."

He gave me a little side-eye. "I hear you. You're going to have to." He pointed at me. "No freebies over here." His phone buzzed. "That's the reception desk. I'll be back. It's our food."

Shit. I think he heard me for real. I know he has my gift of telepathy too. I just feel it. I will have to pay more attention to what I think since I'm not sure if he's as good as I am. But I do want to see if he can hear me how Janet used to.

When the elevator chimed, I made sure I saw him walk into it. I wanted to see what was so important in his special delivery box. It was from Ava Montgomery in Dunwoody, Georgia. He already opened it, so he wouldn't be able to tell that I peeked. I quickly looked inside.

Found these in storage. Thought you might want them.
Ava

There were some books with piano music, real estate books, a watch that looked pretty expensive, a skully hat, and a wedding photo of him and his ex-wife. The back of it said,

Don't forget us.
Ava

The elevator chimed, announcing his return, and I put the box back on the table as he left it. Then I pretended to be scrolling on my phone.

"Well, you can rest assured Natalia was not our delivery girl." He smiled as he opened up the food we placed on napkins. He looked at the box suspiciously and then at me.

I hope I put it back right. *Fuck*.

As he was arranging the food, he said, "Wow, this smells good. So, Journey, where do you see yourself in five years?"

"Rich. Running a wellness empire. Maybe even with two locations."

"Well, anything's possible."

"I have great advisors, so you're right. Anything is possible. My mom's an amazing attorney. I have some great clients that are in business and willing to help, and you, of course." I gave it a shot and said in his mind, *You're going to help me. I want you to help me. You are my best mentor of all.*

He blushed. "I will help where I can, for sure."

Is it working? Wow. I think he did hear me. But I don't think he has a clue of what we can do. I bet he needs a "Janet" to teach him, and since she's not here, I guess I could do it. However, a part of me thinks that I should keep this to myself for now. I don't want to scare him off. I figure I can start small.

"Ty, I know you said you're busy these days with all of your new projects and stuff. You seem to be a little wound up. You should try Yoga one day. I can teach you some breathing techniques and meditation to gain more focus."

"Wound up? Me? Really? I was probably just a little nervous when we first met, and you know this is still kind of new to me. But I'm a Type A personality for the most part."

"Wait? Really? Were you nervous? Papa Bear—that's so cute." He almost spit out his food from laughing.

He pointed at me. "Oh no, don't you ever call me that again." We started cracking up so hard that he had sour cream all over his chin. I pointed to it so he could wipe it off.

"Okay, okay. I promise not to call you that again." I handed him a napkin. "You know I was just teasing you. I would never call you that in public. But for the record, you didn't seem nervous at all. Maybe a little guarded, but not nervous."

"I was so excited that a piece of me was found. You have no idea. You seem to have grown up with a tight-knit family, which I didn't have. Although I have some good stories, it was not always a big happy family. I grew up with a hot-blooded Cuban mother that could throw a plate or *chancleta* at you with the aim of an Olympian discus thrower. And my potty-mouthed Jamaican dad could cuss you out so good you'd wanna cry. The two of them together were great when it was good, but when it was bad—shit. Run for cover." We cracked up.

"Well, most of my family was in Colombia, and even those people didn't treat me the greatest. I felt alone for the most part. So meeting you was one of the best days of my life." My voice cracked, and a tear streamed down my cheek. "Oh hell, I'm sorry. I didn't think I was going to start crying." I grabbed a napkin and dabbed my eyes. "How embarrassing."

"Journey, that's so sweet. Bring it in." He hugged me. I cried a bit more as he rubbed my back and smoothed out my hair. I felt so safe, so loved in my daddy's arms. Finally, I have my daddy. I couldn't wait until he met my mom. It was only a few days away.

Chapter 11

Journey

I was so nervous, and I didn't know why. I mean, Ty and I already had some cool chemistry, but I was freaking out about how Mom would react toward him. She can be a little awkward and cold. My palms were sweaty as I fixed my hair. I just blew it out straight so it would flow down the middle of my back. I put on a nice maxi dress, and I was even shocked to see my mom dolled up in a red dress with lots of cleavage. She hadn't dressed that sexy in years. It's either suits or Yoga clothes.

"Well, look at this hot babe. *Caliente. La dama de rojo.* Who are you, and what did you do with my mother?"

"Oh, hush. I'm trying to make a good impression, is all. I haven't had a reason to dress up in a while. This is a pretty big deal. Look at me. I'm sweating." She grabbed a paper towel from the kitchen and patted her face.

"It's okay. I'm nervous too. You'll love him, though. He's supersweet and kind." The doorbell rang, and we both smiled. I motioned for her to get it.

"Go, Ma."

She opened the door, laid eyes on him, and then she turned to me. Her usual tough exterior went to straight Jell-O. She mouthed, "Oh my God," like a little girl who just saw her crush.

I shouted in the background while I finished setting the table, "Hey, Ty, meet my beautiful mother, Claudia."

He wore a dark suit with a sky-blue shirt. Looked very sharp. I guess he was trying to make a good impression too. "I'm so pleased to meet you, Claudia."

She hugged him so hard. I couldn't believe my eyes. She was overwhelmed. It was probably the guilt of lying to me for so long too.

Her voice was choked with tears. "Oh, the pleasure is all mine. Thank you, Ty. Thank you so much." She broke down. "Oh my goodness. I'm so sorry."

"It's okay, and you're so welcome."

They stared at each other a bit awkwardly in the foyer. I felt like they both were searching for pieces of me in each other's faces. My mom put a quivering hand to her forehead. My eyes got a little watery, so I tried to lighten the mood.

"Wow, check out the waterworks over here. Who knew how happy a sperm donor could make someone?"

My mother snapped. "Journey, behave and have some manners."

He turned to my mom. "It's okay. I've gotten used to her already in the few times we have spent together." We all laughed.

She led Ty to the dining room to sit down, then slapped me in the back of my head playfully. I giggled and hugged Ty. "Dinner's ready. Don't you look spiffy? You are *so* fly."

"Hey, beautiful. Why thank you."

"Ty, I always wondered who she got the wisecrack mouth from."

He sheepishly raised his hand. "I take partial responsibility since I've been known to have a sharp tongue in the boardroom. However, I did hear you were a beast in the courtroom, soooo . . ." he shrugged.

Mom laughed and said, "Well, to be fair, I will take fifty percent of the blame."

"Seeee, so now, you can't blame me. It's in my DNA."

"But you know better. Try that mess with friends, not with the adults."

She took off her apron to show off her dress a little bit more. I peeped him checking her out a little bit.

"Smells good. And what a beautiful home you have."

"Thanks. I've been here most of my life since I was ten years old."

"That's awesome. It looks modern."

"I'm ready to jump the nest."

My mom came in with a plate of food. "Yes, please, jump the nest. *No puedo esperar a tener un nido vacío.*" She looked at Ty.

"You know my Spanish is not that good. Don't start talking about me."

Ty said, "She just said she can't wait to have an empty nest."

Mom looked at him, put her finger over her lips, and laughed.

"Whose fault is that? You don't practice. Why do you think I used to send you away for summers? If you don't use it, you lose it, my love."

"Yeah, yeah."

"Nini, make yourself useful and get the iced tea and the salad."

I got up and walked down the hall to the kitchen. I forgot to make the salad, so it took a little longer than it should have. When I came back, they were laughing hysterically.

"Damn, Journey, I didn't know you were such a little bully."

"Oh my God. What story did she tell you? Ma, what story did you tell him?"

Ty was laughing uncontrollably and wiping tears from his eyes. “Just the one where you had all the little kids in the playground on their knees eating sand, telling them it was cereal you made them.”

“What the hell, Maaaa? I told you I don’t remember that story. I don’t know why you keep telling it.”

She was still laughing. “She was only four.” She turned to me and took a sip of her wine. “Just because you don’t remember it doesn’t mean it didn’t happen. I had to deal with all the parents. The teachers couldn’t believe how she got them all to obey her.” Mom pointed at me. “She’s very persuasive, and she can get people to do what she wants. It was insane. Three of the kids had to go to the hospital for stomach pains. Oh, it was a nightmare.”

“Jeez, sending kids to the hospital? What did you do? Hypnotize them into thinking they were eating Fruity Pebbles?”

“It was pebbles, all right,” Mom said. I couldn’t help but laugh too.

“Well, Claudia, she may very well have inherited that trait from me. The gift of persuasion comes in very handy in business, especially in sales. Runs in the family.”

“Seeee,” I gleamed.

“When you use it in the right way, that is.” Ty gave me a knowing look. I wondered if he really could do what Janet and I did.

I do it all day, Ty. I use my powers for good. I looked to see a reaction.

He looked at me strangely as if he heard my voice in his head, but then he just took a sip of his drink like it was no big deal. Maybe he doesn't know how to tune in just yet.

My mother leaned toward Ty. "So, Journey tells me you've done extremely well for yourself. I'm so impressed and glad I made the right choice."

"Well, my career has not been easy, but I persevered and made the right investments and alliances that helped put my company on the map."

"Journey says she wants to go the same route, at least owning commercial property. She won't stop talking about her idea of her spa or wellness center."

"Mom, really? You said you liked it, and it's a lifestyle center called *A Place for Janet Lifestyle Center.*"

"Nini, you know I love the idea. I just think it's a bit premature. You need to finish college. Then once you do that, I'll take it more seriously."

"College is not necessary for everyone. I just need to finish my business plan. Ty said he would help me."

He nodded in agreement, and I felt so pleased that he was on my side.

Then he cleared his throat. "Well, yes, if it makes sense. If it's something you really can pull off. I'd be interested in looking at your profit margin, what services you will offer, et cetera. Why is it called 'A Place for Janet,' by the way? That's an interesting name."

"It's because I'm dedicating it to a lady I met who was homeless, and we became good friends. I want to honor her and offer programs for those who don't have access to things like Yoga, meditation, etc., things that can improve their mental health. I got her into Yoga, and she turned her life around, but unfortunately, she passed away from cirrhosis of the liver because of her previous life."

"I'm so sorry." Ty patted my hand.

"Yeah, she was an alcoholic at one time. It broke my heart, for real. She was a dear friend."

"That's so sad, and that's a very nice gesture," he said.

"Yes, that's my Journey. She loves helping people. It's a great idea, but I still feel you need to finish school and stop making excuses."

Ty jumped in. "Not that I have any say, but a degree can take you to the next level."

"I'll see. I just feel good about what's going to happen. My hunches have been on point lately. I feel this idea will make millions."

My mom raised her eyebrows and sipped her wine. I don't know if her nerves were bad or what, but I've never seen her drink more than she ate before. "Well, Journey has always been a creative young lady. She has a new idea every week, then gets bored and comes up with another one."

"That's so not true, Ty. She is making me look like some airhead." He's not going to want to invest in someone like that. She really was fucking up my whole idea.

"Why are you trying to play me in front of my donor dad?" I laughed, trying to lighten the tone, but I was truly annoyed.

"Well, last year, it was a recycling business to help save the oceans and rivers. Oh, a few months ago, it was something to help juvenile delinquents with art therapy and Yoga. Then you had this obsession with the lady from the coffee shop . . . Janet. It spiraled into your mission for getting the homeless people off the street," she laughed. "If I would have let you, you would have a shelter in the basement right now. Oh, let's not forget you helped Natalia too, but she turned out to be a good friend. And that husband of hers was a nightmare. He could have killed her."

I began to clench my jaws. She was talking way too much. Ty saw that I was getting upset.

"Very altruistic soul you have. That's beautiful that you have such a huge heart, Journey." He smiled. His eyes were so gentle. He knew my mom was being an asshole.

I looked at my mother angrily. *Shut the fuck up. Spill your wine. Spill your wine and go. Goooo.* She took a sip, and the glass slipped and spilled all over the front of her dress.

"Ay, Dios mio! I must have butterfingers." She giggled nervously and jumped up, patting her dress with a napkin. "Maybe I need to slow down on the wine."

"Yes, maybe you do. What was that, your third glass?" I tilted my head and widened my eyes at her. Finally, she got the memo.

"Oh, hush. Let me go clean this up. I'll be right back."

I tried to hide my smirk, but I think Ty saw it. After that, I continued talking as if nothing had happened.

"You know, I can still do all of those things my mother mentioned, but now as individual programs tied to my lifestyle center, I can even get government grants for things. I feel like A Place for Janet will be the hub for a lot of community events too. I just want to do my part to help make the world better." My face lit up with joy. "You might not see the big picture yet, but I see us all there cutting the ribbon on the red carpet, and guess who's going to be the first one bragging?" I pointed to my mother. She was walking back into the dining room with a big wet spot on her dress.

I stood up and banged my fork against the glass. "Can I have everyone's attention, please? Can I have everyone's attention? Yes, yes . . . I am Claudia Salazar, Esquire, of the Salazar and Steinberger firm. I'm also the mother of Journey Salazar, founder of this magnificent new lifestyle center that is changing lives. Welcome, everyone."

"Oh, stop it." My mother laughed, and she was turning red because she knew damn well that's exactly what she would do.

We all were cracking up. "Ty, I swear, she's always trying to make fun of me, and then when I do something, and it turns out great, she's the first to brag about me."

"Now, *that's* funny. You know moms worry a lot, but they usually are your biggest cheerleaders, right?" He nodded to my mother, who was burying her face in her hands.

"This child right here has an overactive imagination. I just have to pray every day she doesn't make me crazy."

"You mean crazier?" I said.

Mom rolled her eyes at me, now sipping water, and asked, "Do you have any other kids besides the donor ones?"

"Oh no. I don't have any other children. I'm divorced, but we didn't have any kids."

"Well, you got at least three others that seemed pretty cool from what Journey says. Do you plan on meeting those kids?"

I kicked her under the table, and she jolted back and made it so obvious.

Ty's smile turned into a frown of confusion. "What?"

"Oh, I thought you spoke to the others."

His strong posture collapsed like the wind was taken out of him. The loud sound of his knife and fork dropping onto the plate startled me. "No, tell me—what do you mean? What . . . what . . . others?"

I tried to clean it up. "Mom, stop insinuating you know everything. He has a lot of kids out there." I rolled my eyes at her and shouted in her mind. *Stop talking. Just stop.*

He saw my expression, and I couldn't hide my fear.

She stammered. "Journey, you . . . You didn't tell him?" She crossed her arms, ready to take sides and embarrass me further.

What is wrong with you? Shut the fuck up, Mommy.

Her glassy eyes shined. "Why wouldn't you? I mean, wow . . . They are like your new besties. Ty, she talks about them constantly."

I took a deep breath, and my stomach churned like I was about to vomit. I wondered if the liquor didn't allow my message to get through. It's like she couldn't hear me shouting in her mind. I felt so betrayed, but it's my fault for telling her too much. And when she's drinking, she has no sense at all. She wasn't picking up my cues and was acting like a total airhead.

I
Am
Soooo
Fucked.

Chapter 12

Ty

"What's going on? Someone want to fill me in?" The room closed in on me. The energy shifted from playful to dense.

Journey's jaw dropped. Her eyes shifted back and forth between her mom and me. "Well, I met some of your . . . um . . . some of your kids."

"What? Really? How so?"

"Don't you know about the sibling registry? They have it for all of the donors who had children, where we can connect with our siblings even if they never meet you."

"That must be a new feature. So, why the secrecy? I mean, you couldn't tell me? I can understand if they didn't want to meet me. That's not a big deal."

My throat tightened, and I felt heavy. I tried to remain calm.

Claudia shook her head nervously. She tucked her curls behind her ears. "Yes, that is something you should have disclosed with him, Journey." She looked at me and said, "She's been talking with them all the time for a few months now. It's pretty amazing how fast they bonded, so it makes sense that they're connected. They really act related."

My stomach turned. My voice got deeper. "So, they knew that you met me already?"

"No, no . . . I didn't tell them yet. I just . . ."

The fear of meeting three more children started to brew. I felt myself getting angrier, and my voice got louder. "This is already really hard for me to do, and now you're telling me you're connecting with three other kids, and you're keeping it a secret at that?"

"I didn't lie. Why are you tripping, Ty? It's not like you didn't know you had a bunch of kids out there anyway."

She shrugged nonchalantly, and that made me even more furious. I continued eating to calm myself down before I would say something I'd regret.

Claudia said, "Well, she just omitted the truth. Don't you think it would have been nice to tell him how you bonded with them, how you all have the same lips, and even your personalities are the same? It's pretty amazing." Claudia seemed to be clueless about how frustrated I was or how she was blowing Journey's cover.

Journey's voice was low. "They weren't ready to meet you yet."

I was so overwhelmed, and I could tell she was still lying to my face. "I just don't understand why you wouldn't share that with me."

Her guilt was seeping through her pores. "Well, I can set up a call with them if you want to meet them." She got her phone, and when she pulled it out, I saw she had a photo of me on her screen saver with the words My Daddy in hot pink letters over my picture.

"Wow." I blushed.

"Oh, that's nothing. I was just so happy to meet you."

My hands started to shake. Anxiety took over. I didn't know how much longer I could stay there, so I figured I'd end dinner early.

"Listen, I guess I thought I was ready, but this is just too much. Too much dishonesty for me if we're going to be friends. If we're going to have any kind of relationship, I'd prefer honesty, no lies, no sneaky behavior. I'm not trying to step in and be your father, but I was open to a friendship."

Journey shook her head. No words came out of her mouth, but I heard her in my head for some reason. It was almost as if she was shouting at me in a pleading tone. It was as if I were reading her mind, loud and clear.

Don't leave! I didn't want to share you. You're my father. I don't want to share you. It shook me. I felt chills down my back as tears streamed down her face.

Her voice cracked. “I’m sorry, okay? I’m sorry. I won’t do it again. I’ll tell you everything. I’m so sorry.”

I stood up and wiped my mouth with my napkin. “Hey, I think I’m going to get going. Claudia, it was an absolute pleasure.” I took her hand.

Claudia held on to my hand. “Wait, let me talk to you. Don’t leave just yet, please.”

“OK, good night, Ty. I give up!” Journey stormed off to the bathroom. I could tell she was holding in her tears when the door slammed. I couldn’t get out of there fast enough. I don’t do drama, and I don’t do liars. She has become obsessive with me too.

Claudia followed me out. She walked me to my car and talked softly as if she were afraid Journey would hear her. “I assumed you knew. I had no idea. I had no idea she would keep that from you. I’m so sorry.”

“No, I knew nothing. Like, why hide it? That was just bizarre.” I wiped my forehead.

“Listen, you will learn Journey is not always logical. She’s always been a unique and strange child, but she can also be manipulative, even calculated at times. I think she just wanted to build a bond with you first before sharing you with the others.”

“Honestly, Claudia, I just don’t think I’m ready for all the mind games. But I am not going anywhere. I will just take it slow. It was a pretty big bomb to drop on me.” I shifted back and forth.

"Just give her a chance. She's still a kid, and I guess this is all new to all of us."

"I will, but I'm going to take a little break from all of this."

"Can you take my phone number down so you can call to keep in touch?" I handed her my cell, and she typed in her number.

I know she meant well, so I told her I would stay in touch. She was a little flirty and assertive for our first meeting. I took it that she was hoping this was going somewhere. She definitely exuded sex appeal and was a strong woman, but I was not going there. She's a little too old for me. I'm sure she's in her early 60s. And even with all those strengths, she still seemed afraid of Journey.

"This might be a little personal, but . . . but does your family have any issues with mental illness by any chance? Sometimes I wonder if she struggles with something like depression or some sort of personality disorder because she goes back and forth so much."

"No, not that I know of." Huh . . . mental issues? That was cause for alarm.

Claudia glanced at the house uneasily. "Well, full disclosure—she hasn't been diagnosed or anything, but I just feel there's something there, so please, just be easy with her. She's not good with rejection. It's gotten her into trouble in the past. Sometimes, I worry about her. Having a mother as an attorney has saved her in a few instances, and she's improved over the years with therapy. She can overreact at times. I think that's why she never had a boyfriend for long. She can be a bit bossy."

"Really? Like what kind of trouble have you saved her from?"

"Oh, you know, I probably overstepped. It might be best that she shares it with you when she's ready—nothing crazy, just stupid teen stuff. Let's just say she's had a few close calls. She's going to be upset with me, so I just need to shut up. Please, take your time with her. She means well."

My whole energy just shifted. Journey definitely had a sneaky, dark side to her, and I didn't know if it was mental illness or what, but whatever it was, I needed to pull back for a while.

The Next Day . . .

Natalia came into work a little early to help me close a deal. She was close with the local cell phone store owner looking to get a new location in the downtown area. Natalia made the introduction, and we found a place for him to purchase. She represented C&C with class and professionalism.

I was so impressed as we walked out of the location. The sun was shining in my eyes, so I reached for my shades in my blazer pocket. "Natalia, you're a class act. Very well done. Mr. Franklin said he wants to buy it 'as-is' with no problem. That was the easiest deal we made in a while."

"Why, thank you, Ty. I'm trying to make my mark. This is what I love to do."

"And it shows. You know what? Let's celebrate. Let me take you out for an early dinner."

"That's so nice of you." She looked at her watch. "But tonight? I have to—"

"Nonsense. You're your own boss with that Uber Eats stuff. Don't worry about it. I'll pay for whatever you normally make at night. Let your hair down, and let's have some fun to celebrate your achievements. You work hard and deserve to play hard and celebrate. This was a huge deal with them purchasing this location."

"I know. I'm still in awe that it happened. Mr. Franklin said he wants to franchise and open three more stores within the next two years. So, if we stay on track, he'll use us again, and I'm sure he will. I'm thrilled we got someone from the community too."

"Yes. Good deal. You are doing it, girl." I high-fived her. I was looking forward to spending more time with her. She was a prize for our team, and I wanted her to know it. I took her to my favorite steak house in Buckhead. We sat in a secluded booth in the back, and I ordered a bottle of white wine. We raised our glasses, and I said, "Cheers for your first referral. I'm delighted you are on the team."

"Thanks, Ty. I'm so glad to be a part of it."

"Listen, I know that we met through Journey, but I have to keep it one hundred with you. We had a slight falling out last night at dinner. I'm sure she told you already, though." I searched her eyes for a sign. She looked shocked.

"Really? No, she didn't tell me anything. So what did she do?" She looked afraid to hear my answer.

"Did you know about the um . . . the other siblings? The ones that she's made friends with in the last few months?"

"What *other* siblings? You mean like your donor kids?"

"Yes. Her mother said she talks to three of them almost every day on video chat." I reached for the steak sauce and shook some over my tender sirloin.

"Oh, wow. That must be the 'Fantastic Four' she's always talking about. They are a group she met online that are like psychic kids or something." She shook her head in disbelief. "They're not her siblings. They're just some kids she practices all her abilities with. She made it sound as if she were teaching them."

"Well, that's what Claudia told me. There's a thing called the sibling registry from the sperm bank I donated to. I looked it up, and it's a thing. You can find your sisters and brothers made from the same donor. Shit is wild. They've added some things since the nineties when I signed up."

"That's crazy. Are you sure? I would think she would tell me that. What in the world?"

"Exactly. Between you and me—she's called me five times today. I've been letting it go to voicemail. I'm feeling a little overwhelmed about the whole thing. I told her I needed a break. I was really in shock last night. Just a lot of things her mother told me. I gotta say, they made me a little nervous. She even had my photo as a screen saver. It kinda creeped me out."

"Yeah, I saw. Just a little obsessive. I figured it was because she was so happy to have a father figure in her life. But what's so crazy is that she's acting like everything is fine. She even told me that you met her mom and had a great time at dinner last night."

I rubbed my temples and grinned. "Yes, we did . . . until that bomb was dropped on me. Claudia assumed I knew about the kids and just blurted it out. She had a bit too much wine and was telling me everything. It certainly took me for a loop. I mean, it's not like I didn't know I have other kids out there, but the way she handled it was just kind of unsettling to me. I was so uneasy, and I couldn't play it off, so I decided to leave instead to avoid an argument. As you get to know me, Natalia, you'll see I don't do drama, and I have a low tolerance for BS."

She dabbed her mouth with her napkin. "Understandable. Wow. I am so sorry. I'm really in shock. I hate to know you guys are not speaking. Maybe she didn't want to overwhelm you with the new kids just yet, you think?"

"It's possible. She claims they weren't ready to meet me yet. But I don't know what to believe.

Even her mother warned me about the control part. And it's almost as if she were afraid of Journey."

"I've seen it too. Remember, I lived with them for a little bit. Journey has her way with her mom, even though Claudia will try to act tough sometimes. She's pretty spoiled. You gotta realize that was her miracle baby, her only child."

"Who manipulates her. I can see it."

"Journey can be a little bit of a brat because her mom allowed it. I know as a teen, she put her mom through it. I heard the stories—running away, shoplifting. Stuff like that. It's always the privileged kids that want to act up. But she turned out okay. I have to thank them both because my ex would have left me homeless or killed me if I had stayed with him going through a divorce. So, I do owe her my life, in a sense, which is why I put up with a lot of her foolishness at times. And I have to remember she's only twenty-two. Listen, Journey can be a lot to handle. She's overbearing sometimes with her control issues, but she has a good heart. Just be easy on her." She put some more food in her mouth and said, "Ooooh, this steak is delicious. Soooo glad you brought me here."

"It is delicious, nice and tender." I smiled as she excused herself. We had a lot of wine, so Natalia left to go to the bathroom. It started to sink in, everything she was saying about Journey. I guess I could have handled that a bit better. I began to feel a little bit guilty about being so cold toward Journey, so I finally decided to text her back.

***

Sorry if it seems as if I'm ignoring you. I'm a little bit busy. Just give me some time. At dinner with Natalia. Your girl sealed a great deal today for C&C. Hope you're good.

When Natalia came back, she looked so peaceful. So naturally beautiful. Her red lipstick had worn off from the food. She took off her blazer that revealed more of her body in her sexy pink summer dress that hugged her hips and made her body sing to me. I looked at her caramel skin and just smiled. She caught my wandering gaze taking her all in.

"What?" she giggled. "It's hot."

"Oh, nothing. You are just stunning." I cleared my throat. "I mean, just beautiful inside and out."

"Why, thank you. You're not so bad yourself, boss."

"Come on, don't do that. Don't do that." I raised my hands in surrender. "Making me feel like a creepy boss now. I'm sorry. Maybe I said too much."

"No worries. Stop it, Ty. You take yourself too seriously," she laughed. "What do you think? I'm going to report you to HR? It was a nice compliment, and I'll take it."

I sat up straight and fixed my jacket sarcastically. "Now, we will keep it professional." I cleared my throat and smiled.

"As hard as it is." She looked down and fidgeted with the napkin in her lap.

"What's that, Natalia?" I snickered.

She sighed. “I mean, it would just be my luck to meet my friend’s dad, who is pretty much a great catch . . . I mean, I enjoy working with you and your company. You’re such a cool dude and just an upstanding individual overall.”

“Wow, that’s so kind of you to say. You are pretty special too. I enjoy working with you as well. I think you’re pretty brilliant. Are you seeing anyone?”

She grinned. “No, I’m just dating. Nothing serious. Why?”

“Oh, just curious. So, what’s the dating scene like now? I’m still pretty rusty. I could use some tips.”

“You need tips from me? That’s funny. But, it’s not hard to find a date. It’s just finding a *quality* date; that’s the issue. You just got to get on a dating app. It’s so easy. There’s soooo many.”

“Yeah, I’m a bit of an old-school geek. I like connecting in person, not just swiping. You know, I like things to happen organically, naturally.” I was giving her a hint, and I’m sure she knew it, but she wanted to play along.

“Well, I can understand a man of your stature, so you can’t put yourself out there too much. But you can have a vague profile without putting all of your business in the streets. You know, not using your full name for starters. Not using any photos that have been used online already or in the press because people can search those now and link it right to your business.”

“Wow, I didn’t know that. Can you help me?”

"Wait, is this a part of my job?"

"No, no. It's just to help a nigga out." I started laughing, and she almost spit out her wine. "Oh my God, you are crazy."

"No, I think we just might have had a little bit too much wine. I'm sorry. That was rude. The drinks have loosened me up a little bit."

"Oh no, that was funny as hell. Let's get some things down for your profile." She pulled out her phone to take notes. "You got lucky, Ty, since I am the master of making profile pages. I help a lot of my friends get boyfriends. However, it hasn't worked out for me just yet."

"That's because you need a *man*, not a boyfriend."

"Facts." She pointed at me and chuckled. "Okay, so what's your job title? Never mind, we'll just say business owner and keep it vague. If you say you're an investor, the gold diggers will come running."

"Oh yeah, good point. Hell no, don't put that down."

"Okay, the next set of questions will kind of help people see if there is chemistry with your lifestyle choices. What are some hobbies that you like?"

"I love running, hiking, basketball, and traveling. Oh, you know . . . put in swimming. I like swimming too."

"Wow. You ever been to Comet Trail? I love hiking there."

"Yes, it's beautiful."

"What's your level of education?"

"A master's degree."

"Body type . . . wait. I know that already." She looked me up and down and squeezed a bicep. "Hmmmm, definitely, definitely athletic."

"You got me blushing over here."

"What are some of your pet peeves?"

I scratched my head and rolled my neck back and forth, stretching it. "I think that's pretty easy. I don't do stinky weaves, long-ass eyelashes, women with no ambition looking for a sugar daddy, terrible teeth, poor grammar, and women who are not punctual."

"Boy, you sure are specific, but you just locked out fifty percent of Atlanta women."

"Damn, you know you cold-blooded, but that's funny."

"Do you smoke or drink? That's an easier question. We know that you drink. So I'll just put social drinker for that one, so you don't look like a drunk."

"What-you think I'm a drunk now? I'm hardly drunk."

"No, no. I'm just teasing, but do you smoke?"

"No, I don't smoke any cigarettes, but . . ." I shrugged, "I do dabble in the green stuff for stress relief."

"Fair enough, I'm just putting no, but if you want, you can add 420 friendly."

"Wait, that's a thing?"

"Sure, people say it all the time. Especially if you're looking for a smoke buddy."

"Nah, let's leave that out until I get to know the person. That's way too much information for a dating site."

I tilted my head. "Do *you* smoke, Natalia?"

"Well, on rare occasions. Celebrations and such. Maybe like New Year's or my birthday. I've done cigar bars too. But no cigarettes. I'm more of an edibles girl, to be honest. Helps me sleep."

"Well, aren't we celebrating?"

"Ty, what's on your mind?" She slapped my arm. "You are so bad tonight."

"What? You're grown, right? I got some in my car." I raised my eyebrows. "Let's have a few celebratory puffs. Be bad with me."

"Okaaaay, wow. I had no idea this night would go there. I like this side of you, Ty. You're actually a lot of fun."

"Oh, you ain't seen nothing yet," I winked.

I was feeling her. I know, I know—totally unorthodox behavior. Marlon would kill me, but more because I know he wanted her too. Our flirting was moving in the right direction, so I knew she was down. She was trying to be ladylike and professional. I felt a good vibe with her, and I knew we were going to make tonight special. I held up my hand for the check.

We went to sit in my truck, and I drove around the back to a secluded area by some trees. A few puffs in, and Natalia was certainly loosening up. Of course, the wine in her system helped too.

"Oh, this is some good stuff. I feel it in my head more, and my chest is kind of burning." She coughed and laughed at herself. The smoke left her nostrils, and she slowly closed her eyes, enjoying her high.

"California-grown, baby. I know the growers too."

"Of course, you do."

"Only the best for you." I winked as I blew smoke out of the window.

She smiled and spoke so softly. "Ty, you are the best boss ever. And you have the nerve to be fine too." I passed her the blunt, and she took a slow puff and let the smoke escape her mouth really sexy-like.

She was turning me on. I turned to her and said, "Oh yeah, you think so? You're not so bad yourself."

I looked at her legs, and I got so hard. I put the blunt down in the ashtray, and before I could make a move, she leaned in and kissed me. Not just any regular kiss. She was ravishing me, moving her tongue so sensually, sucking, tugging on my bottom lip, kissing my neck. I didn't think she would be so bold. I was not ready to be attacked like that, but I was not complaining. I was pleasantly surprised since I'm usually the aggressor. Natalia was so uninhibited. She almost came over to the driver's side, caressing my neck, my legs, and my chest.

"Damn, mami, I didn't think you had it in you." I came up for air. My hands explored her breasts and felt her hard nipples piercing through her dress.

"I'm sorry. I'm . . . I guess I just held back. I mean, under the circumstances and all." She pulled away.

"No, don't be sorry. I've been building up the nerve myself." I grabbed her hand and put it on my hardness.

She smiled. "Damn, boss. Jesus Christ. What do you got up in there?" She giggled.

I grabbed her chin and kissed her deeply, and she caressed my dick. I wanted to fuck her right there in the backseat. I pulled away and looked into her eyes. Then I grabbed her face. "I like you, you know?"

"Yeah, and I like you too."

I squeezed her inner thigh and leaned in close to her ear. "Can we keep this between us?"

She nodded. "Yes, of course. You think I'm going to tell Journey? Never."

"Okay, look, there's a W Hotel around the block." I raised my eyebrows, waiting for a response.

"Oh, okay." She bit her bottom lip like she was unsure. "Are you sure? What about Papa? Don't you have to be home soon?"

"I'll just give the nurse a call. She stays on weekends, so we should be good."

"I was supposed to work tonight, though . . ."

"Look, I'm not gonna force you, Natalia. I just . . . I mean . . . The way you were coming at me, I figured you were down."

"No, no, I am—"

"Okay, stop worrying about working tonight."

"Are you sure?"

I turned the car on. "Now, let's go before you change your mind." I smiled.

"Oh, I won't." She rubbed my thigh.

"I got some gummies in the glove compartment if you want some."

"Edibles too? Wow, you're really trying to get me fucked up."

"Only if you want it."

"Oh, I think I want it all." She giggled as she went into my glove compartment.

Chapter 13

Journey

Fuck, why is this happening to me? I pray, I meditate, I journal daily to manifest my intentions. I do Yoga every day. Now, my connection with Ty has gone to shit because of my stupid-ass mother. I felt like I was out of control. I just found him. We just finally connected after I was lied to all of my life, and now, it's all going to shit over something so small. I should have just told him, but I wanted my own time alone. I wanted to cherish being the *first* donor child that he met. Introducing him to the Fantastic Four crew would be too much for him. Now, when I called to apologize about him finding out the way he did, he just sent me to voicemail. I feel so rejected. I was too embarrassed to tell Natalia what had happened.

At 10:00 p.m., I got a random text from Ty, and my face instantly lit up. I was pleasantly surprised. He apologized for being distant and said he was busy but then said he was having dinner with Natalia. Wow. Okay, dinner? Without me? He said in his text she got some deal or something, so I guess he wanted to congratulate her. I hope she is doing her job with plugging me good and getting information about his company. I need her help even more now since I know he doesn't trust me. I hoped we could all work together someday soon, bringing A Place for Janet to life.

I was dying to speak with her to find out how dinner went. I wanted to know if he asked about me and what she said. So I waited until about midnight to call. I figured they would have finished by then and that she was already making her late-night deliveries for Uber Eats. She was usually pretty busy on a Friday night at that time. When I called, though, I got her voicemail.

Hey, you, congrats on getting that deal. You are doing the damn thing, Nat. Call me when you get home.

I was surprised she didn't reply, but I know when she does Uber Eats, she has to use her phone and GPS, so she probably wouldn't be able to see it until later. I texted her around 1:30 a.m. Still no reply. My stomach felt squirmy. I started to pace back and forth in my room. My spirit told me something was off. I was worried, but I just couldn't put my finger on it. I hope she wasn't in a car accident or anything crazy.

I called Ty—no answer.

I called Natalia again—no answer.

I know I could just be jealous of their friendship. I do have an overactive imagination. I just hope Natalia is okay on the road. She usually calls me right back or at least texts me immediately.

Suddenly, I heard Janet's voice in my head. *Do what you do, pretty girl.*

"Okay, okay, Janet. I'll try," I said to myself. I missed her so much.

I lay down and started to breathe deeply to calm my nerves. The lavender walls of my room soothed me to relax, but then my heart started to hurt. I didn't want to do it, but something told me I was right. I said her name in my head, *Natalia James, Atlanta, Georgia. Take me to Natalia James, Atlanta, Georgia.*

In an instant, I felt like I was floating over her like an eagle circling her, and I saw a man with her. The room was gray and blue. I couldn't make out who the man was just yet. I heard them panting and groaning. Sighs of passion filled up the room. I looked to my left, and I saw her propped up on the couch, doggie style, and a tall Black man had his pants around his ankles penetrating her. I took a deeper breath to see further. I had to know. Every time I got close to seeing his face, it would blur out. I got a headache from straining. Something dripped on my leg, and I realized it was blood. Shit, my nose was bleeding. Janet did say that could happen sometimes. I couldn't see his face, but I saw his tattoos on his left forearm, and then I knew. It was almost as if I was in denial and did not want to see it. I felt like I was going to be sick. I didn't want to believe this shit.

I called Robbie for a second opinion in case my jealousy was getting the best of me. He was one of the best in the crew, so I knew he would help me solve the mystery.

FaceTime Call

He picked up. He was in a dark room with flickering lights on his chocolate brown face. "What you calling me this late for? You know, I'm your biological brother, right? Don't be calling me at booty call hours." All I saw were his white teeth. He was just a playful jerk.

"Come on, knock it off. You know I wouldn't call you this late unless it was important."

"Okay, what's going on, sis? You good?"

"No, no—not really. I need you to double-check something for me, and uuum, it's kind of urgent."

"It's like one a.m., yo. The spirit guides are off the clock. I'ma have to charge you to wake them up."

I whined, "Come ooon, Robbieeee. It's serious. Can you see if my friend Natalia is with someone right now? But I have to tell you something you might not want to hear. I want to know if she is with Ty."

"Ty? Fifteen forty-four Ty?"

"Yeah."

"See, I knew you met his ass already." He shook his head.

"Don't be mad at me," I pleaded.

"Mad for what? It would be stupid for you not to meet him. You are like the only one that lives in his state anyhow."

"I know. I was trying to find the right time to tell you all. Can you keep this reading between us, though, please? I'll tell Zack and Elizabeth everything tomorrow."

"All right. So, why would Ty be with Natalia? Isn't that your homegirl who is like a big sister? Let me find out pops is a sugar daddy."

"Well, yeah. She's my friend, but she's a little older than us, and I got her an internship with him."

"Word?" He jerked back from the phone dramatically. "Damn, so this has been going on for a while? When'd you meet him?"

"A little over a month ago. I'm feeling sick because I saw a vision of them having sex. Like, what the fuck? My stomach damn near made me throw up. I need to check to see if I'm just making shit up in my head. I can have an overactive imagination."

"Wow, a little over a month, huh?" He shook his head.

"What?"

"Nothing." Robbie sat up in his bed and took a deep breath. "Okay, what's her name?"

"Natalia James in Atlanta."

He closed his eyes and lay back again. "Wowzers. Hot damn, she got a nice body."

"What? Is that what you see?"

"I'm just messing with you. Hold on." He put the phone facedown. I heard deep breathing. "Oh boy. I felt so many emotions coming from her. She's been through a lot, huh?"

"Yeah, she had an abusive husband."

"Damn, no wonder I feel her energy is so in love with Ty. She has a big crush, at the very least. I see them, and they're still together—like right now. I asked my guides, and it looks like they have a strong connection." He picked the phone up to look at me. "Yo, her heart is fluttering so fast. The way her energy feels in my body is crazy. I think she just got fucked by daddy, yo." He laughed loudly.

"No, noooo, that is so wrong and *not* funny."

"Come on, I mean . . . It's her body. Let her live. Isn't she older than you, like thirty-eight or forty?"

"No, she's thirty-two, but it's not the age. It's just that she's my friend. Like, how the fuck could you go there and not think it's going to affect *me* in some way? And I *specifically* told her not to do anything with him. I knew it. I just knew it."

"You don't know the whole story. He's an older, good-looking nigga with long-ass pockets. He probably got a lot of game too. Ain't no female turning that down. Helloooo."

"But she is *my* friend—my *best* friend. That shit is some ho shit. Like, who does that? Fuck their friend's father?"

Robbie threw some more bass up in his voice. "Let's be clear, Journey. Come on, bruh, you just met dude. He's a regular dude and hardly a father. He was a donor—*a donor,* Journey. He was number fifteen forty-four. Stop making up more of a happy family scenario in your mind. It's a fucking fantasy."

"Damn, you gotta be so harsh? It's just the principle of it all."

"Nah, I can't wrap my head around this one. Natalia is a grown-ass woman, right?"

I nodded.

"She's your friend, and you love her, correct?"

"Yeah."

"So, why you cockblocking?"

"It's just weird. I don't *want* them to be dating. Some things are just better separate. That's my dad . . . our father."

"So, it's weird for her to get a millionaire boyfriend? Shit, I ain't mad at her hustle. I could understand if she was your age, but come oooon."

"They are ignoring me like I'm some kid."

"Because they know your irrational ass. At least she does. He might not know you yet." He laughed. "So, look, here's what I saw. They were at a hotel. It looked very sterile and not like somebody's house. No pictures or anything. It looked like they were still doing it or just finished. Is Ty tall?"

My heart raced. My palms got clammy. "Yeah, it's him."

I didn't want to hear it. Ty could have at least respected me by not going there. I grabbed my keys off my dresser and walked slowly to the garage door. My mom had fallen asleep since 11:00 p.m., so I tried not to make too much noise.

Robbie saw me moving around.

"Journey? Journey? Where are you going this late?"

"Nowhere. I just need to get some air. I gotta get out of here. I'm pissed." My voice cracked. "I don't know. I just feel weird. I need air. I'm gonna go for a drive, that's all."

"Lies. How you going to lie to me? For real?" He pointed to his chest. "What you 'bout to do, girl? Your brother can read your ass. Yo, Journey, look at me."

I wrestled with my keys and picked up my purse. "Yes, Robbie?"

"Do some of that deep pariyamma breathing you Yogis do."

I snickered. "You mean pranayama breathing? You are so silly. I love you. Thank you for the reading. I got you next time, but I'm feeling sick." I jumped into my car and slammed the steering wheel.

"You shouldn't be driving when you're mad. No . . . like, for real."

"I'm good, I'm good. Just driving around the block." The garage door was so loud I hoped it didn't wake my mom.

"All right. Hit me tomorrow. If Natalia tells you what really happened, I want to hear the story."

"She probably won't."

"I know. All right, peace."

It was so dark, but the stars and moon shone brightly. I drove slowly to Natalia's apartment complex in silence. The anger began to build inside of me. Just like that, the old me came back. When I pulled up to her spot, her car was not in her parking space, just like I thought.

"That little ho couldn't keep her panties up."

Chapter 14

Ty

Natalia's brown eyes sparkled from being high and a little tipsy. Her shy and dainty act went straight out of the window once those substances kicked in and pulled back a layer on how she truly felt. The second I opened the hotel door, she showered me with more kisses and started to unbutton my shirt.

"Natalia, I . . . oh . . . Wow, you're not playing, but I just want to make sure. Are you sure you want to do this?"

She grabbed my hands and put them on her ass. I pushed her up against the wall and started kissing her back. I lifted her as we continued to go at it.

"I'm positive. I was trying to be good." She kissed my neck, "But you make it soooo hard."

"You don't have to pretend anymore." I picked her up, walked her to the bed, and reached under her skirt. I rubbed her hips and thighs. Her body was so soft and warm.

She asked, "You got condoms?"

"Of course. They were right next to the gummies in the glove compartment."

She took off her blouse and started unzipping my pants as she sat on the edge of the bed. I prayed she could keep this a secret, but I felt it would get out eventually because I see her being more than just a fling. Without a doubt, I was digging her. I stood in front of her, and she stroked my dick in my boxers and then pushed them down to my knees. She took me in her mouth in one fell swoop and played with the head, rubbing it between her breasts. They were so soft and plump. They didn't even look like they were that big in her outfits. I had no idea she was packing what looked like a double-D cup. I was so excited. I couldn't believe this was going down. She was full of so much passion. Who knew?

I pushed her back on the bed and got on top of her to slow her down a bit. She was pretty aggressive. I wanted to run the show. I spread her legs and played with her clit while kissing her and sucking on her neck. Then I went down on her and gave her all I had . . . my tongue. It was driving her wild. She moaned in delight, which turned me on even more. Her voice was so gentle in my ear. I nibbled on her inner thighs, and just when she relaxed, I ventured in again and buried my face deep inside her.

Natalia clenched my head. "Ty, why you teasing meeee?"

"Shhhh. Patience. Just enjoy it." I took off the rest of my clothes and stood over her for a minute.

"Damn, you look so good naked." I bent down and sucked on her breasts. She kept opening her legs even more. I loved how much she showed she wanted me. She could not wait.

"Oh, you want this dick, don't you? I see you squirming." I slapped her spot lightly.

"You play too much," she giggled.

"I don't know if you're ready. Can you take it?" I rubbed my fingers over her pussy lips. "It looks pretty tight down there, mami." I jerked my dick slowly and then put on a condom while looking at her.

"Yes, I can tak–" I got on top of her and eased into her so deeply. She was so wet anticipating me. She moaned so loud. "Fuck, ooooh my God."

She felt so good. So tight. I guess she hadn't been with anyone since she broke up with her ex. I felt like I was fucking a virgin. We were grinding into each other at a nice pace. We had a lot of pent-up passion from the first time we met. I'd been fantasizing about making love to her for weeks.

I eased off her and took her hand. "Come here, beautiful." I led her to the balcony.

"They can see us," she whispered.

I turned out the lights so no one in the building across the street would be able to make us out clearly. Then I pushed her down over the balcony. Natalia held on and gasped as I entered her and started to slowly stroke her. The city lights illuminated the sky and gave me the perfect view of the downtown Atlanta skyline. I looked down a few floors across the street and noticed someone was on a hotel balcony watching us while they smoked, but I didn't care.

"Ty, this feels so good. Oh my God."

"Do you like it?" I grabbed her throat to pull her face to mine. "I can't hear you. Talk to me."

She moaned something inaudible. "Yes. Yes . . . I love it. You fuck . . . me . . . so . . . good. I love this . . ."

Just her voice made me want to come. I was so turned on that my body was vibrating.

"Oh, you're so sexy. You are so ah . . . aaaah." Her neat bun came out, and her hair was suddenly wild and free. I grabbed it, and Natalia gave a loud yelp.

We started giggling and could not stop. The weed definitely kicked in and gave us the giggles. It was contagious. The guy across the street pumped his fist toward me to salute me. It made me laugh even more. I did not tell Natalia. She would have been mortified.

I said, "Come back inside. We're too loud. Someone might report us."

We fell onto the bed giggling hysterically.

I imitated her yelp sound. "Yelp, ruff, ruff. Yo, you sounded like a barking Chihuahua."

"I know, like one that just got kicked. You took me by surprise. I love my hair being pulled, though, just as an FYI."

"Oh, do you?" I playfully yanked it. "Duly noted. I'm glad it didn't fall off in my hands."

"Oh noooo. It's all mine. Otherwise, I would have warned you not to touch it."

"I want to touch you all over."

She crawled on top of me and started kissing me. "You are so good. I thought Jamaicans didn't eat coochie."

I smirked. "That's a myth. I'm closer to the Spanish side of my family anyway. We eat pussy with bread." We both laughed. I pretended to sop up a piece of bread in between her legs.

"Oh my God, you are so silly." She cuddled on my side and whispered, "So, what now?"

"I'm diggin' you. Let's just keep it on the low for now, but I don't think I need to make a dating profile just yet."

"Shoot, you thought I was going to help you make one after all this action?"

"You are really special, Natalia. Let's take it slow."

"Okay. I'll follow your lead, Ty. You're the boss."

***

The following day, I had absolutely no regrets. However, I think Natalia may have since she received over twelve text messages and phone calls from Journey. I ordered room service, and while we were eating breakfast, she turned her phone back on and saw all of the texts.

She looked at her phone and then looked at me nervously. "I think she knows."

"Oh, come on. How could she know? Stop worrying."

"She's texting me. 'Oh, I know what you're doing. That's fucked up.' I don't even want to call her."

"Just wait until you get home and tell her you met someone. She's bluffing. She doesn't have a clue. I'm sure she knows you date. She's just fishing. You might have to remind her that you're an adult."

"She said, 'I know you're with Ty,' though." The look of fear in her eyes was unreal.

"Shit, that might be partly my fault. I was feeling a little guilty after talking to you, and when we were at the restaurant, I texted her and told her we were at dinner."

"Oh, so that's how she knew."

Natalia looked so afraid like Journey was her damn mother. What is it that she does that has everyone so scared? She's just a damn kid.

"Look, at the end of the day, you're grown, and that's your vagina, not Journey's." I rubbed her back gently. "Well, I want it to be my vagina too. At least on weekends."

Natalia almost choked on her eggs. We cracked up. "I still feel high, you know? You?"

"Nah, you a lightweight. Or you just high off of me."

"Whatever. So uuuum, back to us. If she asks me, I'll deny it."

"Dat a girl. Let's take it day by day, and if it comes to us telling her in the future, I will be there with you."

Natalia's phone rang again, and she looked at me. She showed me her screen of Journey's face on it.

I shrugged and sipped my orange juice. "Just answer it."

"OK, I'll get this before she has a damn heart attack." She stepped away to sit on the balcony, but she didn't close the door, so I heard every word. I continued eating my bacon and eggs like I wasn't paying attention, but I was.

"Hey, Journey, why are you talking crazy? What? What is wrong with you? You're wrong. I had a date. Yeah, someone new . . . What are you, my mom, now? Stop freaking out like you control him.

He's not your dad. You just met him . . . No, noooo. I'm not diminishing the connection, but come on, Journey, you just met him. You are acting so possessive it's embarrassing. You gonna scare him off . . . Well, you're wrong. Yeah, you too."

Natalia got up from the balcony and screamed, "Would you believe she hung up on me? She's losing it. Yelling and saying, 'I knoooow you fucked my dad.' She said I'm a liar."

"That's crazy how she even thought that."

"Well, she's no dummy. She peeped how you were checking me out when we first met." She smoothed at her dress and smiled at me.

"Oh, you mean how you were sweating me hard?" I pointed to my chest and flexed my muscles. We started laughing. I had to do something to lighten the mood. I felt terrible for putting her in the middle of things. We were both nervous about Journey being overly dramatic, but I tried to downplay it.

After breakfast, I dropped Natalia off at her car and headed home. I had such a good time, even with all the distractions. I called Marlon. He had to hear this shit.

"Yo."

"What up, doh. What's good, Ty?"

"Look, man, I'ma just go ahead and say it. You were right. It happened."

There was an awkward silence. "Wait—what? Ah, man, no no no. You fucked that girl, didn't you?"

"All night," I laughed.

"My niggaaaa, I knew you couldn't keep your dick in your pants. But what now? You going to keep her on board. That can be messy, bro."

"I don't think so. She's got a head on her shoulders. I like her mind. She's a keeper. We good. She's stable. Not like them loco chicks you be pulling."

"Ah, come on—ain't nothing like a little crazy pussy. Those be the best."

"I've had my share . . . Don't want my Maserati keyed up."

"You lucky Journey is your daughter, 'cause I would put a hurting on her fine young Latina ass."

My voice got low. "Hey, Marlon, watch it."

"Yeah, that was out of pocket." He snickered. Sometimes he gets carried away.

"And she's mad young too, you damn pedophile. Natalia is grown." I cleared my throat. "But speaking of Journey, she really showed her age last night *and* this morning."

"What she do?"

"She was blowing up our phones all night. I told her I was taking Natalia to a work dinner, and she just accused Natalia of fucking me. Like, what the fuck?"

"Well, she was right," he laughed. "I told you, son. It's them witchcraft genes you got. She probably do the same shit you be doing: seeing things, walking through walls. Aaaand she's a female, so you know how it is on level ten with them. They got that woman's intuition."

"Man, please, but you may be right." I looked at my caller ID on the dashboard. "You are not gonna believe this. Guess who calling me right now?"

"Ah, shit. Better get your story straight. She ain't gonna wanna hear you were slaying her friend last night. Or *all* night, as you put it." He laughed. "That's just messy."

"I'll handle it."

"Soooo you say. A'ight, get that. See you at practice later. Don't forget. Peace."

"A'ight. See you there."

I answered Journey's video call and tried to remain pleasant.

"Hey, Ty. Soooo, how was dinner?" She had a knowing smirk on her face.

I ignored her question. "Hey, Journey. How are you?" I was pulling into the garage and just parked my car.

"I'm great. I see you had a good time. Just getting in?"

"Huh? What, are you keeping tabs on my schedule now?"

"No, I just know you had my girlfriend out all hours of the night." She was beginning to act like a jealous girlfriend. It frightened me just a tad. Journey had a phony smile plastered across her face.

"Really? I think that's a bit of an exaggeration. We just had dinner celebrating her win. Is that what she told you?" I couldn't believe I was even explaining myself to this kid.

"No, she didn't tell me. She denied it too, but I know you both are lying. It's all good, though. You could have invited me."

"Journey, you need to watch your tone. Look, I'm busy right now and headed to my gym to work out. You don't have to keep tabs on Natalia or me. We're adults." My eyes widened. "And to be honest, your behavior is freaking me out."

"Oh, sorry. I didn't mean to blow your spot up like that. I was hoping that we could meet up. I had a surprise for you."

I sighed. "Actually, no. Today is pretty busy, and I think I need some time after what happened at dinner and all."

"I apologized 1,000 times, Ty. And the surprise is now ruined since that's why I wanted to meet up so I can introduce you to the others on FaceTime."

"Yeah? I don't think I'm ready, Journey. I'll give you a call when I am. I got a lot going on, and honestly, I can't be in your life like you want me to."

"But they are your kids, and they want to meet you too."

"Yeah, and apparently, you were trying to hold me back from them. You only had a change of heart because Claudia spilled the beans. And let's be clear. I'm their *donor,* and it's my option, not an obligation, to make connections with you or any of them."

"Wow, you got cold-blooded on me." She laughed a nervous laugh as she paced around her bedroom.

"I'm sorry if I'm coming across that way, but I just really can't handle all of this right now. You're making it a little difficult by being so aggressive. So let's just take it one day at a time."

She gave me an evil look, and I felt it to my core. "Fine, I'll leave you alone until you're ready. Have a nice day, Tyler."

She hung up, and chills ran down my back. Maybe I was too harsh, but her stubborn ass doesn't get it. I had to rip off the Band-Aid and tell her the raw truth. Her mother was without a doubt trying to warn me, so I think I'll fall back for a while.

Chapter 15

Journey

Guilty. Guilty as charged. I called him on FaceTime just to see his lying eyes. Ty seemed like he couldn't even park his car right because he seemed so disturbed that he could feel my accusing eyes staring him down. I couldn't believe how cold he was toward me. Like he was a total asshole to me. I just wanted him to tell me the truth. It's almost like Natalia told him stuff about me and turned him against me. He was blowing me off like I'm a nuisance and not his seed. He told me he would help me. He promised me he would help me, and now he's treating me like an afterthought. When I asked him if he and my friend were out all night, his ass looked so shook. It's so apparent too since Natalia has been avoiding me all morning. At first, I pretended I was worried about her.

I called her a few times last night and then went to voicemail.

1st text: Nat, where you at?

2nd text: Are you okay? I haven't heard back from you.

That little ho. She just had to do it. I should have known when she kept talking about how fine he was that she was going to give it a shot. And Ty was just as bad as her. Like, how could you? You know that's one of my friends. By the seventh time of calling her and getting her voicemail, I just left her a message.

"I know you are ignoring me, Natalia. I said to flirt with him. Get him to help me with my center. I even got you that job. But noooo, you just had to fuck him, didn't you?"

After speaking to them both this morning, I knew what Robbie and I saw was the truth. And you know, it's not even the fact of the matter that they fucked that got me so upset. It was facing the reality that he would find the time to spend with her now when he could be getting to know me more. Yes, I was jealous because it just wasn't fair. My plan was falling apart. I wanted him to be close to me and work on being a father to meeee. I got something for him, though. He might not want to help me anymore or be there for me, but I know someone who will.

***

I got a text from Elizabeth saying we needed an emergency meeting ASAP.

Video Group Chat—Fantastic Four

They called me on a group chat as if they were already talking about me.

"Soooo, heard you met our dear old dad." Elizabeth looked at me with a smug face. I was already in a bad mood and not ready for the ambush.

"Yes. I was going to tell you guys."

Zack said, "Yeah, like a month later? That's fucked up, Journey. We are supposed to be in this together. We are family. Those are *your* words."

"I know. Damn, Robbie. I thought you were gonna let *me* tell them."

Robbie confessed. "Look, they needed to know. That's not something you could keep hiding from us."

"He's planning on helping me build my lifestyle center. Ty is really cool, guys. He wants to meet you all soon too. When I open up A Place for Janet, we can all work there. There are so many people hurting and need healing. We can teach classes. I want it to be a place for transformation."

"Do you even hear yourself, Journey?" Robbie said.

Zack chimed in. "I don't think she does, dude. I think you have a bit of a god complex, Journey."

Elizabeth said, "I hate to say it, but I have to agree. We are studying narcissism in my psychology class, and you fit the bill. Speaking of which, you never even did our readings for us."

"Okay, okay. I'm sorry y'all feel that way. Shit. Is this 'jump on Journey' day? God complex? Really?"

"No, it isn't jump on Journey day." Elizabeth didn't flinch. "It's time just to be honest with us. I'm starting to feel like you are just using us."

I never saw so much attitude in her.

"I'm sorry. I haven't been the best sister. A lot has been going on, and it's just been a bit overwhelming. I'll do better, I promise. Let me just get through this day."

Elizabeth softened her tone. "Look, we love you, but you gotta see our side of things. We know sometimes you mean well, but you just have to be a bit more considerate."

"I will admit that I have been a bit damaged by my mother's lies, and I just wanted to hold on to him for myself for a minute. I didn't have stepdads raise me like you all did. I was going to tell you all soon. I swear." My mouth quivered, and my eyes started to water. I hated them judging me.

Zack rolled his eyes and sat back on his couch. He wasn't buying it.

"I'm sorry. Do you guys want me to set up a call with him?"

"Yeah, that would be great for starters," Robbie said. "I wanna meet this dude who is dropping panties. Maybe I can learn a thing or two."

"Dropping *what?*" Elizabeth jerked back.

"Oh God. Really, Robbie? That does not even sound right. Well, yeah, he is messing around with my friend, Nat."

Elizabeth yelled, "Natalia? The one you call your big sis? Yikes. Scandalous."

Zack smiled. "Damn, he moves fast. Okay, Daddioooo." He and Robbie laughed. They would have high-fived in person, I'm sure. Jerks.

"I'll talk to you guys later. Sorry again for not telling you sooner." I hung up, not even waiting for their goodbyes. That shit was not funny. I felt attacked. They were probably all gossiping about me now. Fuck it. I'll win them back once I get Ty to come back around too. A phone call with them all will be good. It will help everyone see the truth. I'm not a bad person.

Chapter 16

Ty

It's been a week since Natalia and I have been intimate, and the whole Journey situation freaked us out. It truly had spun out of control. Journey hadn't called or texted me since we had our little talk, and she pretty much hung up on me. Natalia said she's been avoiding her calls, but they had it out too. It's evident that Journey struggles with some kind of mental illness or temper issues. I'm not sure which one, but something is certainly off. The obsession with controlling others has to be one of those disorders. Marlon told me that she even called him for advice on locations and to get more information on the company. I thought that was very odd. I do remember him sliding his card to her. Since she couldn't talk to me, she just went around me. He said he could tell she was trying to make more connections to be closer to me. But she was going about it all wrong and making herself look desperate and ridiculous. One thing I learned is never to reward bad behavior.

Well, today was a big day. I looked in my hallway mirror at my purple and black basketball uniform, and I felt proud. The championship was finally here, and we were going to win it.

"Good luck today, Mr. Carter," Jocelyn said while she propped up Papa's legs on the ottoman.

"Thanks. I'll see you when I return."

"If you win, I'll have a special surprise dinner for you."

"Oh, thank you. I want dessert too," I winked.

"No problem. I got your dessert too." She puckered her lips to me where Papa couldn't see.

"I can't wait to come back."

"Have fun."

I was rushing out the door and looked up at the overcast sky. The gray clouds moved slowly and gave me an eerie feeling. I hadn't heard from Marlon when he was always the first to call me early in the morning to hype me up about how we were going to kick the next team's asses. When I got to the gym, no one had heard from him either. I called and texted him but still nothing. I was going straight to voicemail. The game was in fifteen minutes. He couldn't be that stupid to have gone out to a party Friday night. He knew better. Something didn't feel good in my spirit since Marlon never missed a game. I knew the second the game was over, I needed to check on him. I only dropped 12 points without Marlon, my point guard, a.k.a. my hype man. We ended up losing by 10 points. I was devastated. We worked so hard as a team and were so close to victory.

After the game, I checked my phone and received a text alert from my bank saying that the business account was down $5,000, which was very bizarre since we had no expenses last week. I jumped on I-85, doing ninety mph. I called again and again on my way to his house and still got no answer. My heart was racing as I ran up the stairs of his townhome. As I knocked on the door, I had this feeling of dread in my stomach. No one answered, so I rang the bell. The window blinds next to the door started ruffling as if someone was watching me.

"Yo, open up, Marlon. You okay, man?"

The door creaked open, and I couldn't believe my fucking eyes. It was Journey. She opened the door slowly. Her lips parted slightly and framed an evil smile.

"Journey? What are you doing here? Where's Marlon?"

"He's asleep. What's wrong?" Her voice was soft, and her smile—sinister. Her hair was frizzy and unkempt as if she had had a wild night. I was in absolute shock. "What the hell are you doing here?" I looked down and saw she had on one of Marlon's shirts and no pants. I felt sick to my stomach.

I pushed past her. "Marlon!"

"Jeez, Ty, why are you so mad?"

I went to the back and found him facedown in bed.

"Ayoooo, Marlon! Marlon, wake the fuck up." I hit his back, but he didn't move. The worst thought crossed my mind. I looked back, and there she was, leaning in the doorway with her arms crossed, gloating. "What did you do to him?" I yelled.

"What did *I* do? You should be asking what did he do to *meeee*. Oh, but then again, don't ask me shit. I'm grown, and you're not my daddy—just a donor."

"Oh, is that what this is about? Really? Please, put some clothes on. I can't even look at you." She left the room.

"It's too loud, it's too loud," Marlon mumbled as he turned his head slowly toward me.

I bent down and shook him. "Oh, it's about to get louder, my nigga. Wake the fuck up. Did you lose your fucking mind, bruh? Smashing Journey? *Really?*"

Marlon was muttering some incoherent words, and he grabbed my hand so tightly. "What's going on? What are you doing here?" Then he saw Journey walk back into the room. Now she was in a tight purple dress, drinking a glass of water.

"Oh no no no." He shook his head. "Oh, man, it's not . . . It's not what you think, Ty. She wanted me to help her with a surprise . . ."

"I don't give a shit." I punched him in the jaw. He screamed in pain. I grabbed him by the shoulders. I was livid. "What is *wrong* with you? She's a damn kid." Now, I punched the wall behind him. I wanted to kill him.

He pushed me off him. "Chill, man, chill." Marlon sat up, holding his jaw.

Journey chimed in, "Ty, don't hit him. I'm grown. I'm twenty-two, for your information. He didn't force me to do anything I didn't want to do."

I cut my eyes at her. "Journey, please, get out. I'm not talking to you."

"Maybe I deserved it. She's very, very convincing." He whispered, "Real talk, I think she drugged me, man. I don't know what it was, but she had to have drugged me. Please get her out of here. Like now." His protruding eyes told me there was way more to this story.

"Journey, what did you give him?"

She moved in closer to us, casually drinking. "Give him? We just had a lot to drink. He's just hungover. Why are you so bent out of shape? You got a big vein popping out of your head," she giggled. "He's a big boy. He'll sleep it off."

"This shit ain't right. I've seen Marlon drunk. This ain't it. What the hell did you give him, Journeeeey?" I slapped the dresser, and my breathing was rapid. I wanted to fling her out of the house and down the stairs.

She just smiled.

"You playing with us? You think this shit is funny? I had no idea you were this diabolical."

"Well, the fruit doesn't fall far from the tree." She pointed to my face. "Yoooou slept with my best friend, so now we can go on a double date together. Fair enough?"

"What? You need some serious help. Get out. Get out! Do you need me to call you a car?"

She flinched a little but tried to remain calm. I knew it was all an act. "No, I drove myself." She looked in the mirror as she talked while throwing her hair in a bun. "I put some coffee on. He'll be fine in a few hours. Stop being a drama king. We just had a little fun. Right, Marlon?" She winked at him. Marlon shook his head and jerked back like a frightened animal.

Her nonchalant demeanor was chilling. I knew she was up to something more.

"Marlon, what happened? What the fuck, man?"

"I don't know what she did, but she drugged me for sure. I don't remember everything, but I know she isn't who she says she is." His pupils were dilated, and he looked like he was on something. I clenched my jaws and thought about bringing her back into the room to question her again.

Journey was in the hallway and yelled in a cheery voice, "Bye, guys. Off to teach Yoga." The door slammed.

Marlon was grabbing his head, searching for memories. As much as I wanted to punch him again, I realized something awful had happened to him last night. I wanted to go chase Journey, but I was so concerned about him. My eyes darted across the room, looking for clues. I saw sheets on the floor, his clothes in the chair, empty wineglasses. It looked like a regular wild night, but one thing stood out to me. Marlon's money clip was sitting on the dresser, empty. He always kept this lucky hundred-dollar bill. He had it for years. His credit cards were spilled out around the dresser too.

"Did she ask you for money? Tell me what happened."

"I . . . I don't remember. I don't know."

"Marlon, you withdrew $5,000 this morning from our business account. What did you do with that money?" I shook him, but he just had a far-off look in his eyes.

"No. Why would I take any money, like $5,000? Are you sure? I haven't left this bed. Look at me."

"That's it. I'm calling Journey, and if anything, I'm going to the bank, and then I'm going to call the fucking cops."

He tried to stand up. "No, no. Please don't call her back here. Shit, I feel so dizzy. What did she do to meeee?" He held his head and sat back down.

"Why are you so afraid of her? What the fuck is wrong with you? She's only a twenty-two-year-old kid. You're acting like a damn pussy. Get up and splash some water on your face. Wake up. We gotta figure this shit out and fast."

He took a deep breath. "She makes you do stuff. She's powerful. She's like a master. A master. She's not who you think she is. I kind of remember. Last night, she was asking a lot of questions. Pictures. She took a lot of pictures too." He slapped his temples. "And . . . and she kept talking about these other siblings, how she was gonna set up a trip. Oh, man, I know now she wanted to fly them in. They were in other states or something. Shit, I remember her asking for money for that. But I don't remember giving her the money. What the fuck could she have given me to make me lose my memory? I feel so dizzy. Like this is a nightmare. It's so foggy."

"Do you remember what you drank?"

"Oh, wine. It was my wine. But we weren't supposed to be here. We were at the office at first. Yes, yes . . . I remember we were originally going to meet at the office, and then somehow, we ended up here. She drove."

"Yes, I was wondering why I didn't see your car. I thought maybe it was in the garage."

"No, she drove. She was supposed to be just passing by, no more than twenty minutes, she said. So we got to talking, and time passed. I had some wine and offered her a glass . . . yo . . . oh fuck. Is today the game? Oh shit, is that time right?" He pointed to the clock on the wall. "It's not fucking one o'clock, is it? Noooo."

"Yes, today was the game, Marlon, at nine a.m. That's why I came here looking for your ass. We lost by ten points."

"No . . . noooo . . . We lost? What the fuck? How did I sleep through all of this? It's like I lost time. What did she give me, a freaking sleeping pill? I know it looks bad. I'm so sorry, Ty. I know it sounds like bullshit, but I couldn't stop her." He whispered, "She has some kind of mind-control thing. It's like that shit that you do, but it's like that on steroids." He looked panicked, and his hands were shaking as his memories flooded back in. "I didn't have control over myself. Maaaan, she is dangerous—so dangerous."

"I see that now. Without a doubt, I see that now. I've never seen you like this."

I called Journey's cell, and it just went to voicemail. I needed her to admit to what she did.

Marlon's voice was shaky. "My throat. It's so dry. I know she gave me something. I just don't feel right. It's not liquor; it's not a hangover . . . it's . . . it's something else. I should not have let her pour my drink."

"Where's your lucky hundred dollar bill?" I pointed to the dresser.

"Fuck. She musta took it. I had more money in there. Almost a grand. That little bitch."

"Come on and get dressed. We're gonna handle this shit today. She's not going to get away with this."

Chapter 17

Journey

The Evening Before . . .

Men will always be the weaker sex since they think with their dicks. I figured Ty wanted to be mean to me and block me out of his life like I don't exist, fuck my friend, and then lie about it. So, I had something for him, and he was not ready for it. I had Marlon's number from when he gave me his card at the game. I knew I was going to need it at some point. I just had no idea why.

"Hi, Marlon. This is Journey, Ty's daughter."

"Hey, love, I know who you are. What's happening? What a nice surprise."

"Oh, I'm calling you about me . . . me and Ty. See, I recently told him about some of my other siblings, and he was pretty upset with me. Well, it was the way he found out. I didn't tell him. My mother did."

"Yeah, I heard about that, but are y'all okay now?"

"No, not really. He's hardly speaking to me. Like legit ghosting me. I wanted to know if we could meet up to talk about it. I want to know more about how I can make up with him since you are his best friend and all. I have some ideas and maybe will even set up a meeting with the other kids."

"Oh, that's a tough one. That might not be a good idea as a surprise. Ty might not be ready for all of that, and once he makes up his mind about something, he can be pretty stubborn."

I want to see you now. Let's talk today. You know you want to see me, Marlon. Make it happen. I need your help, I said in his head.

I wasn't sure if my powers worked as well over the phone versus in person, but I figured we would see. So I talked a little sweeter and laid it on thick. "Do you have some time today by any chance? I can meet you at the office so that it's not inconvenient for you. I just want to plan something special to make it up to him with your help."

"Sure, but I might have to leave early. I can only stay until about six or so."

"I won't be long, maybe twenty or thirty minutes. I need the address."

"No, that's cool. I'll text you the address."

"Great, thanks for making time for me, Marlon. I truly appreciate it. I'll be there. Please keep it a secret." I smiled at my reflection in my bedroom mirror. That was easier than I thought. I felt my belly flutter. I was ready to have some fun.

I wore my tight purple dress that was a head-turner when I hung out. It accentuated all my curves and made my ass look fat. Kendu used to love it. I would do all that I could to get what I wanted, *especially* to get my revenge. Am I petty? Maybe—I saw how Marlon was flirting with me when I first met him. Men like him were easy to control. Their dicks are the bigger and more vulnerable brains that ruled them. Dummies.

When I got to the office, he laid eyes on me in my dress, and I already knew I had him. I wore my hair in a tight high ponytail and did my makeup light and sultry.

"Wow, look at you looking like a superstar. Where are you going?"

"Oh, thanks. Girls' night—we do it almost every Friday," I lied.

"Well, damn, them young boys ain't ready."

"Oh, I don't deal with young boys," I said matter-of-factly.

"Well, excuse the hell outta me." He laughed nervously. I knew he loved my boldness. "Come on in." His hand was on my waist as he led me into his office. "How can I help you?" His eyes went from my breasts to my hips and my legs. He didn't even try to hide it. "Have a seat." He patted the chair next to him as he sat down.

"Well, I wanted to know if you could help me get back in good graces with Ty. He's mad at me right now, and I'm so sad about it." Marlon nodded along as I spoke. "I was trying to wait before I told him about the other siblings because I didn't want to overwhelm him. I mean—he knows he has other kids. He just didn't realize I had a relationship with them already. My mother blurted it out, and now he's upset with me as if I were sneaky or something, and that wasn't my intention. It kinda blindsided him."

He exhaled. "Just give him some time. He can overreact. This is all new to him. And that is a big blow to know you had a whole crew of his children you're friends with."

"I just met him, and I don't want to lose him already. Can you please help me? What can I do?" I touched his hand softly, and he seemed to melt. "I think once he meets them, he'll be very pleased. Let me show you this picture of them."

I went into my purse and took out the photo. Inside of it was the powder I needed to finish the job. I got it from my last trip to Colombia. When I opened up the paper, I brought it closer to Marlon's face and blew at it while I held my nose.

Marlon looked confused. He stared at me for a minute, then sneezed. "What was that?"

"Are you okay, Marlon?"

"Yeah, what was that?"

"Oh, nothing. Some dust or makeup powder spilled in my purse. I think we need to go to your house to talk some more, right?" I stood up slowly in front of him in between his legs. *You know why I'm here. I wanna fuck you. Don't you wanna touch me?*

He stared at me in a daze. His lips parted slightly. I was in awe at how powerful a teaspoon of Devil's Breath powder could be. This was my second time using it, and it was even more potent than my gift of telepathy. Devil's Breath, also known as scopolamine and burundanga, was one of the world's most dangerous drugs. I just put it in an empty shampoo bottle on my way back from my last visit, and not a soul knew. I wanted to see if it lived up to its reputation. The first time I used it on Phil, and that's how I got him to pay for my Yoga website to help create my lifestyle brand. It was like it made him a mindless zombie who did what I commanded. The best part is he didn't remember shit the next day. He probably would have done it without it, but I wanted to test it on somebody.

My heart raced. "Marlon, Marlon. What do you want to do . . . to me?"

His demeanor was very calm. He looked up at me and rubbed his hands up my legs and around my ass. He was a handsome chocolate man, but even so, I was going to have fun and not get caught up. I bent down and almost kissed him, but I didn't want any of the powder on me. "Why don't you go wash your face and then let's go. I'll drive."

"Okay. You'll drive?" He looked confused.

"Yes. Just tell me where." I didn't want to risk him driving and still under the influence. There's no telling what could happen.

After coming back from washing his face, he said, "I'm feeling a little funny."

"That's okay. I'll make you feel better. Come here."

Marlon was about six feet one, and he smiled and came close to me. I kissed him gently on his lips.

He backed away. "Wow, wow. We probably shouldn't."

"You let me worry about what we should and shouldn't do."

I lightly brushed my hand against his hard imprint. "Marlon, I knew you wanted me. Don't worry. It's our little secret." I rubbed my hand up and down his dick.

"I do want you. I do. I feel a little light-headed, though."

"Let's go. You can sit down in my car," I whispered in his ear. "I want you to fuck the shit out of me, Marlon. Can you do that?"

He nodded his head fast like a little kid being offered the whole cookie jar. He was so calm. I loved how quickly that drug worked. No wonder the prostitutes in Colombia use it so regularly. Oh, tonight, he was gonna be *my* bitch. At first, I just wanted to play with him, but I got such an adrenaline rush after feeling what he was packing that I might want to ride that dick.

We got to Marlon's townhome, and I was impressed. It was almost as fly as Ty's spot. It had a cozier feeling to it. Ty's house was more like a fancy hotel penthouse. Marlon's spot had French doors, warm colors, high ceilings, and lots of plants. He probably had one of his girlfriends help him design it. Felt like a family lived there.

"No one is home, right? You live alone?"

"Yes."

I thought I'd see just how much he would listen to my commands.

"For the rest of the night, I want you to refer to me as 'Master.' Is that okay with you?" I smirked, holding in my laughter.

His eyes were glassy, and he nodded in agreement. He looked so stoned. Shit, with Devil's Breath and my telepathy powers, I could take over the fucking world. I was getting such a rush from it. I wish I could tell someone, but it was a secret I was gonna take to the grave. Not even the Fantastic Four would know. I only had a few hours before it wore off, so I had to work fast.

I sat on the edge of the couch. "Take off your clothes, Marlon."

He looked confused as we were in the living room. “Here?”

“Let’s go to the bedroom,” I said. He led me upstairs. The room was huge and oval-shaped with silver and white decor. A large crystal chandelier hung over the bed. Very classy.

His energy was not the cocky comedian I remembered. He was quiet and stared at me in awe as if waiting for instructions. It was kinda eerie. He was like a robot with a big dick. I couldn’t stop smiling.

We walked into the bedroom, and he started to take off his shirt, and then he went up to me to try to kiss me.

“Did I say you could kiss me yet?”

“No. I’m sorry.”

“No, what?”

“No . . . Ma . . . Master?” His eyes turned down to the floor.

“Get naked.” He began to undress, and I stood there watching him. I was getting turned on by how powerful I felt. I mean, this guy was one of the most influential millionaires in Atlanta, and with one blow of dust in his face, I got him to bow down to the queen. I was having way too much fun. It was making me horny too. I sat on the bed and propped myself up with my elbows as I gave out commands.

My voice was stern. “Take your dick out. I wanna see it.”

He pulled down his boxers, and his body was very nice with a slim build like a track star. Strong biceps, ripped abs, and nice, muscular legs. I had no idea he had all of that going on under his suits. I beckoned him to join me on the bed with my finger. "Come here. You are soooo sexy."

He crawled on top of me, and I started to kiss him. He was really into it.

I stroked his hard dick, "Ooooh, I want to remember how beautiful it is. I'm taking a picture."

He just nodded. I reached to the floor for my purse to get my cell. "Stand up in front of me. Yes, just like that." He stood over me, and I snapped a photo of him holding his rock-hard dick.

"Wait, this one's for you." I got on my knees and started to lick and suck it with one hand, but I pressed record with the other. I felt so good and empowered doing it. If he ever turned on me, I had collateral.

He moaned so loud. "Oh my . . . whoa . . . whoa . . . This is amazing."

"Who is amazing?"

"You, Master, you are the Master. Damn." He clutched my hair.

I laughed at the camera. "That's right. That's right." I stopped the video.

I took off my dress and threw it to the ground. He stared at me in awe. It was as if his senses were coming back to him. Slowly, he sat on the edge of the bed.

"We shouldn't do this."

"Why not? I'm old enough, and you know you want me. Look at that hard dick." I grabbed it again and slapped it lightly. "We can wait just a little before I give you all of me. There are a few things I need you to do first. It will help Ty too. I want to fly my siblings into Atlanta. I need access to your account. Can you help me pay for it? I can't do it alone."

He nodded as he watched my partially nude body walk around in front of him.

"How much do you need?"

"Don't worry about that. I know you got it. Why don't you write me a check?"

"Right now?"

I tugged his dick lightly. "If you want me, then yes. Get your checkbook now."

He walked over to his desk and pulled out a big binder that was more like a ledger. He wrote a check and signed it but left it blank. I put it in my purse.

"You're so beautiful. Can I have you now?"

"Thank you, and you're such a good boy." I kissed him and straddled him in my panties, and I took off my bra. He fondled my breasts and smiled. I got off him and lay down next to him. "Let's lie down for a bit, okay?"

"Okay, Master. But I want to make love to you. You are so gorgeous."

"You will." I took my cell phone out and took a selfie with him wrapped around me in the bed.

"Why are you doing that?"

"Memories. Don't you want to remember this night? Our first night together." I took one of his hands and put it inside my panties. He started to finger me, and I loved how good it felt. I wasn't going to fuck him at first, but I was on such a high of getting revenge . . . getting some good dick from an older man was the icing on the cake.

"Where are your condoms?" He lay lifeless in the bed and pointed to the nightstand.

I got the box, took one out, and rolled it on him. I couldn't wait to get on top. I straddled him slowly and let him go deep inside me.

He was so in shock that it was happening. I felt like he was going in and out of his zombie stupor. "Fuck, baby girl. You are working it. Shiiiit . . . Journey."

"Not my name." I slapped him lightly on his cheek.

"Master. Master. Ooooh, baby. You are the fucking master," he smiled.

I rode him fast and moved my hips around his dick with a precision that drove him wild. We both were sweating so much from the intensity of it all.

I slowed it down, and he grabbed my ass cheeks. He slapped them so hard, and it sent me quivering. "You are so good. Oh, Master, you are soooo, soooo good. This young pussy, damn. Aaaah." He came so hard and loud.

"Damn, Marlon. Fuuuuck. Ooooh." I started shivering, and then I followed right behind him. My body was shaking. I collapsed next to him, and we both just smiled at each other. After a few moments, I got up and went to his wine cabinet, then poured two glasses of red wine for us. He just looked at my naked body and smiled. I let my hair float over my breasts. We sat up, sipping wine.

He whispered, "Am I dreaming?"

"No, you are not. You just fucked your best friend's daughter. Fucked her well, I might add."

He looked a little shaken but then started to laugh with me as we drank.

I let him drink more than me so that my plan would work. I went to sleep with him but woke up early. He was snoring so hard, so I knew that he wasn't waking up anytime soon. I got dressed and drove to a check-cashing spot that I knew cashed big checks. I made it out to cash for 5K. What was he gonna do? I had video and photos now. I wished he would try me. I would take down their whole empire and put them to shame with the footage I got. It's sad that I had to use him to get back at Ty, but a girl's gotta do what a girl's gotta do.

I was gone for nearly an hour, and he never woke up. When I came back, I started snooping around. He had about $1,000 in cash on his money clip. I took that too. Oh well, he's a millionaire, so that was chump change. I went through his computer and saw what a freak he was. He had photos and porn of a bunch of Asian and white women. Go figure. I'm not even his type.

His snoring was unbearable, so I slept in the living room. I wasn't sure how he would react when the drug wore off, but I knew it did make you feel spacey and forgetful. Either way, he couldn't deny my naked body prancing around his house or the footage I obtained. He was sleeping so long that I went and checked on him a few times to make sure he was still breathing. When I saw that he was, I put his limp index finger to his phone to read his text messages between him and Ty. Most of the convos were business related, but I came across a text from Ty earlier that morning.

7:30 a.m. Yo, man, where you at? We got the game today.

8:00 a.m. I hope you didn't hang out last night, Negro.

8:50 a.m.The game is starting. WTF, yo? Where are you? Hurry up.

12:15 p.m. Why are you not picking up? You okay, man? I'm headed over there.

That was just what I wanted. The fun was about to begin. Oh, I could not wait. Before I opened the door, I stood over Marlon and said in his head, *You won't remember much, but just know I am and always will be your master. Fuck with me, and you'll have a price to pay. The consequences of not following my rules will take you all down. Remember that.*

Then I bent down and kissed him on the forehead. He just shifted from one side to the other and kept sleeping. I'm sure he got the message, though.

That look on Ty's face when he saw me come to the door in Marlon's shirt was fucking priceless. The best part is Marlon was so out of it and still clueless on how much money I got as a "company donation" that I was gloating the entire time.

Punch him, Ty. Punch Marlon in the face. He fucked your daughter.

Yep, that was me too. Yeah, I know I can use my powers for good, but sometimes I just wanna be bad.

Chapter 18

Ty

"Come on, Marlon. We gotta goooo. Let's go. Get dressed." I slapped his leg.

"Are you serious? I can barely sit up without feeling like I'm going to fall over. I'm not able to move much. I need to get that coffee."

"Are you crazy? You're not drinking that. *She* made it. We already don't know what she gave you to make you like this. I don't trust her. I'll order you some Starbucks to get delivered. I'll go by myself. Just stay here and don't let her back in."

"Man, I can't thank you enough. I honestly didn't mean for this shit to happen. I'm so sorry. I'm never going to forgive myself." His eyes were watering.

"Look, man, save your sorries for now. I have to call the bank and head to her mother's to have a little sit-down. Journey's going to stop the madness today."

***

My adrenaline was rushing as I hightailed it to my car. I was beyond furious. How could she take it this far?

I called Natalia on video chat from my car.

"Hey, you," she smiled. "Whoa, what's with the face?"

"Oh, what's with the face? I'll tell you—your little friend not only fucked Marlon, but we also think she drugged him and even stole money from him and our business."

She jerked back and screamed, "What? Journey? Are you serious? Are you sure? That doesn't sound right."

"Dead serious, and I'm praying to God you didn't know anything about it." I started my car and sped down I-85.

"Ty, come on. Who me? Really? Are you sure? I mean, she has money. Her mom has money, at least. And she seems to do pretty well teaching. Why would she steal?"

"Who knows. Your guess is as good as mine. A jealous rage? Mentally unstable? Some people just get a rush from doing shit like that. That's *your* friend. I have no idea who the fuck she is, but I'm finding out very quickly. All I know is $5,000 was missing from our account this morning, and Marlon had a money clip full of money, and now it's empty when he woke up next to *her*."

"That's insane. She really slept with him?" She did look surprised, so I figured she wasn't in on any master plan.

"Yes."

"Wow. She must be on some serious revenge trip. This is scary."

"This shit is draining me."

"I have not returned her calls yet either, so I guess she's just furious with both of us." She held her forehead and cleared her throat. "And you know, I didn't want to say anything before, but I think she might be just a little obsessed with you. Journey even had a picture of you on her phone as a screen saver. I thought that was a bit much. I knew she was happy to meet you and all, but yeah . . ."

"I saw it too. 'Obsessed' is an understatement. Well, after I'm done with her, she's going to want to take me off her phone. Is this something you saw her do before, Natalia? I mean . . . I know she's a little high-strung and jealous. She told me a story about going to some ex-boyfriend's house in a rage, but you know, now that I think about it, she knows how to do that out-of-body experience stuff, so she probably did it to us too, and it made her even angrier.

"She is pretty psychic . . . That makes sense, but this story is a little extreme, Ty. Stealing is so low and drugging him too? You sure Marlon is not exaggerating or trying to cover his ass?"

"Hell no. Trust me, if you were there and saw what I saw, you would know something crazy happened. He was an absolute mess. He looked so lost. Do you know if Journey has ever done drugs or had access to any drug? This is some crackhead behavior, man, especially when you try to steal this much money."

"No, no. She's a health nut. Nothing other than weed now and then."

"Well, Marlon is feeling extremely dizzy, and it's almost like he has amnesia. I've seen him drunk many times over the years, and this ain't it. I'm on my way to her mother's house, and I'm calling the bank as well. If she was the one to steal it, I'm going to the cops today."

"Oh God, Ty, this is so horrible. I'm so sorry. I can't believe she would do that, but please, make sure."

"Five thousand, Natalia, five fucking K. That's a felony, and I don't give a shit if she's my blood or not."

"Talk to her mom. I'm sure she can work it out with you."

"I want my money *and* for Journey to pay the consequences. She's an entitled little girl with a silver spoon in her mouth and has gotten away with probably more than we know."

"This is so fucked up." Natalia ran her fingers through her hair. "Just call Claudia. I'm sure she can get to the bottom of this. I knew Journey had a temper and all, but I never thought she would stoop this low. I'm still in shock."

"Well, if you speak to her before I do, let her know the game is over. The gloves are fucking off. I'll talk to you later."

"Okay. I might just go by the studio and have a little chat with her. Keep me posted. Breathe, Ty, breathe. Please drive safely."

"I will."

I called Claudia, and her cell went to voicemail. I left a message but decided to head over there anyhow. When I pulled up, I didn't see her car or Journey's, so I decided to wait and do a little digging on my phone. I went online and pulled up a background check on Journey. I wish I had done it before I even met her to save me from this drama. To my surprise, she had a record. Three cases of felonies, shoplifting, orders of protection against her, and forgery. What the hell? When I tried to review the details of the cases, I saw that they were blocked and the cases were sealed.

There was no question in my mind that she was a damn thief now. I immediately called the bank. They said a check was made out to cash and was cleared at a check-cashing store downtown this morning around 9:30 a.m. I'm sure Marlon had been dead asleep then, the way he was in a damn coma when I got there. I hit my fist on the dashboard. "That fucking little vindictive bitch."

Just as I said that Claudia pulled into the driveway in her cherry-red Mercedes. She got out dressed in full Yoga gear with her Yoga mat strap across her shoulder, looking as happy as ever. Too bad I had nothing but bad news for her.

As she opened her front door, I hopped out of the truck and lightly jogged toward her.

"Claudia, Claudia, I have to speak with you."

"Oh my God, Ty. What are you doing here? You scared me." She opened her door and took off her shades. "Are you okay? Come on in. What's wrong?"

"I called you and left a message. You didn't get it?"

She put her Yoga bag and purse down on the foyer table. "Oh no, I'm so sorry. I was at Yoga with Journey. She teaches today. My phone was off."

"Well, this news is pretty serious. So you may want to sit down for this."

Her eyes widened with a look of concern as she led me to the living room.

"Oh no. What did she do?" Her shoulders slumped as she sat down.

"Well, she did a hell of a lot. Listen . . . I'm just going to cut to the chase. She slept with my business partner, who is my age, to be exact."

Claudia didn't look even close to being surprised. She chuckled. "Oh, is *that* it? Well, that is Journey. She's a bit of a free spirit. I can't tell her what to do when it comes to that since it's her body and she is of age. Trust me; she reminds me of it often." She brushed her hair behind her ears. "It's probably because she had no father figure in her life, so she always had a lot of older boyfriends."

I couldn't believe how cavalier she was about it.

She continued, "I thought her tastes were changing since the last guy, Kendu . . . He was close to her age, like twenty-three or something. But Journey is just full of surprises. Is it going to make you and your partner have issues?"

"No, no, it's not just that. She also drugged him and stole money from—"

She sat straighter. "Oh no, what? How much?"

It's almost as if this was a thing that she was used to. I couldn't believe how calm she remained.

"How much, Ty?"

"At least five K from my business. We know she stole a check and cashed it. She took some cash from him as well. She did this all this morning, by the way."

Claudia went in her purse and started to write a check.

"How are you not shocked? But, wait, what are you doing? Did you hear what I just said?"

"I'm writing you a check." Her face was stern and commanding. "You want this to go away, don't you? Well, I do too."

I stood up. "No, no—it's not going to go away with just a check, Claudia. Once I finish my investigation and see what's what, I am pressing charges."

She stood up too. "What? She's your daughter . . . you, you can't . . . Why would you do that?"

"Oh yes, the hell I can. She's a thief, Claudia. And I know that night that we met, you tried to warn me about her. I just had no idea of what she was capable of." Claudia shook her head and sighed. "You mentioned mental illness as if you knew something I didn't. Is that what we're dealing with right here? Tell me the truth. What's going on with her?"

"Yes, I think so, but you don't understand. She can't go to jail. It will ruin her life. I've tried so hard to give her a good foundation and get her on the right track."

"And I'm sorry to say, look where we are now." I waved my hands in the air. "It seems to me you enabled her every step of the way. I did a little research today and saw her little rap sheet online. I see that you probably expunged some of her cases and let her walk with a little slap on the wrist. Maybe with some community service, am I right? Ya know, now that I think about it, that's why she's so gung ho about doing community service and helping others with her lifestyle center she keeps talking about. She got plenty of practice. And it's like she keeps hinting that she wants money out of me. I'm no fucking dummy."

"Ty, I'll admit I wasn't always there for her while she was growing up since I was building my career. Because of that, she has made some silly mistakes as a teenager. So, yes . . . Yes, I have helped her out in the past." Her voice softened, "But she is not well. I don't know what's wrong. It's not like . . . like we need the money. She . . . She just goes on these little rampages when things are not going her way." Her brows wrinkled. "I thought she was getting better." Claudia blankly stared at me. "Especially after she met you, she seemed so much happier. I don't know what could have happened."

"Well, get her psychiatric help. This shit is not normal. It's dangerous, and she's out there drugging people. I mean, come on. This is fucking crazy. She can end up hurting someone or someone hurting her. And not to mention stealing is a criminal offense as well. So what more does she have to do to wake you the fuck up? I'm sorry; excuse my language."

"It's okay. It's okay. I understand." She was holding back her tears.

"I just can't wrap my head around all of this. I think what set her off is she thinks that I slept with Natalia. The jealousy started there." I wasn't going to tell Claudia that I actually did sleep with Natalia.

"What? So, tell me. What makes you think your partner was drugged?" She folded her arms and had a restless stance. "Was he feeling disoriented, dizzy, forgetful? Acting kind of strange?"

"Yes, yes. All of the above. He said he had a dry mouth too, but he could have been thirsty. Do you know what it was? Please, tell me. I might have to bring him to the emergency room."

She shook her head. "Ay, *Dios mio*. I think I know. Goddammit, Journey." She sat back down and collapsed her head in her hands. A look of shame came across her face. She spoke softer. "Journey was in Colombia about eight months ago, and I have some unsavory cousins who she was hanging out with for a little bit unbeknownst to me. They . . . They may have given her some scopolamine. It's easy to smuggle since most people in the States know nothing about it."

"What? What is that? I've never heard of it."

"The street name is Devil's Breath. It is like a drug that kind of takes away your free will. It makes you very tired, but it kind of turns you into a zombie or like a slave even, rumors say."

"What? Are you serious? That sounds crazy."

"Yes, and you know, she joked around about buying some to use on guys. But I just ignored her like she was joking. I don't take her too seriously since, you know, she's a comedian."

"This shit is far from funny. Could she have put it in a drink? How do you give it to somebody?"

"She possibly blew it right in his face, on a piece of paper, or put it on his skin or his face without him knowing.

"I can't believe she relapsed. She was doing so well. I thought connecting her with you would change everything, and I guess it did for a little while. When I was sick last year, she was going downhill with depression. I almost thought she was even suicidal at one point. I thought knowing about you would keep her spirits up. I'm so sorry this has turned out to be a total disaster. Please let me just write you a check, and I'll get her some help."

"Claudia, I'm so sorry. I'm not the one to take advantage of. You can write a check, but I want her to pay you back with her own money. And she's going to have to do some kind of time for this. I don't care if it's a week in jail. I want her to learn her lesson. She will never learn if you keep covering for her like she's a baby. If she needs therapy, then get her that. I will speak with my attorney and get back to you on what I decide to do. You can let Journey know. I am done. And Marlon and I *will* speak with the police." I moved toward the door, and Claudia grabbed me, hugged me, and started crying on my shoulder.

"Please, I'll pay you back. But, please, don't send my baby to jail. She won't be able to handle it."

"She should have thought about that before she did what she did. I can't be the dad she wants, but what she will learn from me is that the real world does have consequences." I moved away from her grasp. "I'll be in touch." She handed me a check, and I shoved it in my pocket on my way out the door. "Thank you."

Chapter 19

Ty

I stormed into my apartment and slapped my keys on the counter.

"Well, hello to you too. How was the game?" Jocelyn said as she stirred something in the pot. It smelled like beef stew.

"We lost."

"So sorry. That's why you're so grumpy?"

"No, that and just a lot of other shit going on."

"Oh, okay. If you want to talk about it—"

"No, I'm good, Jocelyn. I'm good." I walked over to Papa and stood behind his chair. "Hey there, Papa." I rubbed his shoulders as he watched TV.

"I guess you should know that he's been crying all morning."

"Crying?"

"Yes, and mumbling things. Not sure what he's talking about. He keeps looking around as if he sees something in front of him."

"Probably just a memory coming up."

I stood in front of him and tapped his leg. "Papa, you over here crying?" He shook his head.

"You know, Jocelyn wouldn't lie on you, right?"

"Music, por favor." He pointed to the keyboard—his way of changing the subject.

Jocelyn teased, "Oh, come on, piano man. He's making a request. Just one song. Maybe it will cheer him up."

I was not in the mood to play, but maybe a few minutes on the keys would calm me down. I was so upset. I sat down at the piano bench and thought of an upbeat tune to make us all smile. I thought I would be funny and play one of his favorite songs. "Lloraras" by Oscar d'León. It means you'll cry in English since he claimed he wasn't crying. It went at a fiery pace and was a fun salsa song, even though it was about revenge on a girl that broke his heart.

Jocelyn started to clap and dance as well as sing along. She had a decent singing voice. The upbeat energy of salsa always made me feel better. She stood in front of Papa and held his hand while she sang "*Se que tu no quienes, que yo ti te quier-aaaaa.*"

Papa started tapping his feet and smiling. Jocelyn began to dance in a circle around Papa, and I looked back and laughed. She played the drums on the wooden coffee table. She was the party starter who brought me so much joy. She helped me release some of the stress of the day. The mood shifted with one song. I felt better, even if just for a moment.

"We should form a band."

I shook my head. "They would boo us."

"Oh, let me finish cooking before I burn up my stew." Jocelyn rushed back into the kitchen.

Papa said slowly, "Thank you . . . Tylercito, gracias."

"De nada, Papa. De nada. No more crying, okay?" He mumbled something and beckoned me closer as if he was going to whisper in my ear. "*La mujer.*"

I got up from the piano so that I could hear him. "Sí, sí, what girl?"

"*La mujer es muy malo.*" He shook his head and grunted. I grabbed his hands. They were trembling and clammy. He had a look of fear in his eyes I'd never seen before.

I whispered back, "*Quien?*" I pointed to Jocelyn, and my worst fears took over.

He shook his head. "No, noooo, *hija es mala.*"

Wow, even he knew, or he must have felt something was off about Journey.

My cell rang, and Marlon interrupted us. He sounded hysterical and out of breath. "You got to call your kid, man! The bitch is trying to blackmail me. She just texted me a picture and a video I don't even remember taking. I swear, Ty, I swear I don't remember doing shit. This is bugging me out, yo. Like my eyes look glassy and shit in the video. I don't look like myself. She was doing the most. You know damn well I protect my rep, and I don't take naked videos and photos. I work too hard for this." He was breathing heavily and sounded like he was about to cry. "She got my dick out, yo. I'm sorry to say this, but she got . . . I can't even say this shit. Ah fuck. She just texted me more pictures. Just look at your phone."

"Are you serious? What the hell? You don't remember anything?" I scrolled to my text, and I felt sick. I won't be able to unsee that shit. It was a picture of Journey's mouth on Marlon's dick. His face was in the picture too looking a bit out of it.

"No, no . . . I don't remember these pictures or even what she was doing. She even got me calling her a . . . Oh, man, Ty." He mumbled something. "I know it's a threat."

"Marlon, calm down. Slow down so I can understand you. She got you calling her a what?"

"A 'Master.' A fucking Master. How high could I have been? Oh, man, you don't want to see this shit. I'ma sue this bitch if she posts it anywhere, you hear me?"

I slapped the wall. "Damn, Journey."

Papa started rocking and mumbling, "*El diablo . . . el diablo . . . el diablo.*"

I turned to him. "Papa, calm down. Chill, Papa." I said to Marlon, "Even Papa knows. He just said the girl is bad, and now he's screaming she's the devil in Spanish. I didn't even tell him anything. This whole situation is unreal. She's a monster! Did you speak to her yet?"

"No, she just texted me all these pictures and videos, and she just ended with the last text saying, 'Play nice.' It's like play nice or else. She won't pick up the phone when I call her. I want to strangle her vindictive ass. Like, what the fuck did I do to her to deserve this?"

"It's not you. It's me she's getting back at. She is so evil and vengeful over stupid shit. I can't wait to get her out of my life. She's making me regret ever donating my sperm. I hope the other kids are not like her. I'll refuse to meet any more of them."

"I-I can't wrap my head around it all. She's putting me in the middle of y'all's shit. Like I don't remember anything . . . like my memory was wiped clean."

"I got news on what it could be. I think I know. I spoke to her mom, and she thinks it's some drug from Colombia. I looked it up. It's called Devil's Breath, and from what I read, it will soon wear off."

"When . . . I want my memories back. I'm missing like half a day, it seems."

"Don't panic. It should wear off soon, from what I researched. It's a real thing—it kind of turns people into zombies. A lot of criminals and prostitutes use it in Colombia. We gotta press charges. I'm coming to get you soon so that we can go to the police precinct."

"What else did the mom say? Does she know her daughter is out of her mind?"

"Yes, apparently she does. She just wrote a check for $5,000, like she can make the shit go away, but I don't care. I mean, she didn't even blink. That little girl is going to learn today. She is out of hand and needs to be taught a lesson."

"I'm scared, man. What if she posts something to get back at us?"

"She won't post shit since she's going to get locked up today. I'm so sorry for punching you earlier, but you gotta understand how it looked to me at first. I mean, who would have thought she was the mastermind behind all this crap?"

"Man, I barely remember you punching me. But everything just makes sense because I'm still wondering why my car was at the office. Tiffany called and said that she came in today and saw my car. So, Journey must have drugged me at the office and drove me here. What a devious bitch."

I looked up at the skyline. The clouds subsided, and the sun was shining so bright. It was such a beautiful day for so much chaos to be going on. "Why she gotta be my child? It makes me sick to know that I could have helped conceive a fucking little monster with no conscience. She might very well be a psychopath."

Papa tapped his slippers to get my attention. "Tylercito . . . please . . . don't . . ."

"What, Papa? Don't what?"

"*No abras la puerta.*" His eyes started to water. Jocelyn was in the kitchen, but I know she was soaking up my entire conversation. Finally, she came out of the kitchen to console Papa.

"The door? Don't open the door? I'm not opening the door. What's wrong?"

"Marlon, let me go. I'ma scoop you in a bit. Drink a lot of water. The coffee should be there soon. Flush that shit out of your system. Don't worry. We're gonna handle this."

"Okay . . . cool."

Papa cried a little more, and Jocelyn was consoling him.

"Señor Garcia, what's wrong?"

She kissed him on the top of his head and rubbed his shoulders to comfort him. "What is he talking about . . . *diablo?* Did I hear him right? Is he talking about your daughter?"

"Yes, a whole lot happened today *and* last night."

"Yeah, I heard. If Papa is calling her the devil, she must be one. She stole money too?"

"She did that and a whole lot more, Jocelyn."

***

My cell phone rang. I put my finger up for silence. I looked at my caller ID, and it was her . . . Journey. Chills ran down my back and arms.

She said in a dry voice, “Hey, I’m downstairs. Can I come up? We need to talk.”

“Yes, we most definitely do.” I buzzed her in. I didn’t want to argue on the phone or tell her what Marlon told me. But, oh, it’s on. I couldn’t wait to hear her bullshit.

Chapter 20

Journey

I stayed late at the studio cleaning. I sprayed the Yoga mats down with essential oils and mopped the main entrance. I smiled, picturing how whipped Marlon was acting. I put it on him good. I saw Natalia waiting in the parking lot as I left the studio, leaning against her car. "Journey, what's going on? Are you losing it?"

I walked over to her with my arms folded. "Who me? Lose it? Oh no, I think it's you that's losing it. I'm doing just fine. You avoiding me all week says it all."

"I've been avoiding you because I'm sick of your ridiculous accusations, and it's just making you look crazy as fuck. So I figured we needed to talk it out in person and not text. From what I'm hearing, things have gotten waaaay out of hand. You are *not* going to cost me the very dream job you wanted me to have."

"Oh, I'm sure you sealed the deal—now after you busted it wide open for him."

"What?" She sucked her teeth.

"I already knoooow, Nat, so give up the front. You really think you can lie to me?" I tapped my temple.

"You need to get some help. I know you longed to have a father, but all this shit is just scaring him away, and now he thinks I'm in on this shit you just pulled. I heard you fucked Marlon. And you're stealing money? What the hell? You ain't no hood rat. Is that true? Why would you do that?"

"Oh, he told you that already?" I snickered. "Y'all are close, huh?" I rolled my eyes.

"You drugged Marlon? Is *that* true? Please tell me that is *not* true, Journey."

I just smiled and crossed my arms. My stomach was churning because even though I was furious with her, I hated that she found out.

"Ty wants to press charges. He said you stole money, like five thousand. Is *that* true? Answer me." She had tears in her eyes as if she felt sorry for me. I didn't want her pity.

"Come on. You *believe* that? I don't need money. Shit, I lent you money. That's all bullshit. Marlon was just scared because Ty showed up at his crib and busted us. He's just a pussy and trying to paint the picture that I'm the bad guy, but he was the one coming on to me since day one. Ty just can't take a taste of his own medicine."

"Really? So, you slept with Marlon to get back at Ty since you assumed he and I had sex? Do you realize how childish you sound?"

My voice cracked, and I raised my arms in anger. "Please, Natalia, cut the pious act. I'm sick of your lies. I *know* you fucked him. I know." I pointed at her face. "I saw it. My brother Robbie saw it. Did you know he's fucking his nurse too? You are just a piece of ass to him. You are not loyal or the sister-friend you pretended to be. That's *my* dad."

"You didn't see shit. Your psychic powers are not always right. You . . . You are so delusional." Her eyes tightened as she yelled, "You are just a lonely, sad person that pretends to be so fucking woke. You are so spiritual, soooo grounded, soooo for the people—but you know what I realized, Journey? All you do is judge and try to control everyone. It's all about me, me, me. You manipulate people, and you think everyone is so naive. But I've been peeping you. You are a classic narcissist. I tried, Lord knows I tried to see the good in you, but now, I'm done. I'm officially *done*."

"Please, narcissist? All I do is help people." I pointed at her face. "If it weren't for me, you would probably be dead from your ex's abuse you put up with. I have done nothing but help you, Nat. And you coming for me like *I'm* the enemy?"

She backed away from me. Her voice quivered and softened. "I know deep down in there you have a good heart. However, something went totally left the second you met Ty. I see it, and I appreciate how you helped me when I was down, but I don't know who you are anymore. It's frightening." She shook her head and sniffled, fighting back the tears.

"What do you mean? I'm still the same."

"No, no, you're not. And if you think the word hasn't gotten out about you turning tricks like a whore at the studio, trust me, people are talking. I didn't want to believe it, but now I'm fully convinced the rumors are true."

"Rumors? What rumors?"

"Not worth repeating." She clicked her alarm for her car and opened the door. "Ty is a good man, and it's a pity you can't be more like *him*."

My hands were trembling. I held on to the door and told her to roll down the window. I looked into her eyes and said in her mind, *Tell me what you heard. Tell me now.*

She took a deep breath. "One of your students said her man was paying you weekly for sexual favors. He confessed when he got busted. She saw his bank statements. Now, they're getting a divorce because of you."

"Who said that?"

"Philip's wife, Helen. I bumped into her at Whole Foods, and she told me everything. She warned me about you."

"That is *not* true."

"Journey, I hope you find your way, and I hope you make it right with Ty because I'm done."

My chest tightened as I watched her wipe a tear from her cheek. There was a thickness in my throat that wanted to get in the last word, but before I could, Natalia rolled up the window and drove off.

I stood there speechless. I wanted to cry, but I sucked it in. I turned around and noticed another teacher was sitting in her car listening to the whole convo, pretending to be looking at her phone. Fuck. I hope she didn't hear that. She waved when we made eye contact. I just faked a smile and got in my car. My chest felt like a dagger had pierced it. I didn't want to lose Natalia, but I think there was no saving that friendship. She was disgusted with me, and I was with her, so I guess we're even. I will try to patch things up with Ty. The least I can do is try.

When I got in my car, my mother called me panicking. She said Ty came to the house complaining about all the things I did. Of course, I denied it all and told her Marlon gave me the money as a donation for A Place For Janet. I said he was on board and wanted to be a part of it, and he's just ashamed that Ty found out about us. I was pissed when she told me she already gave him a check to repay them. That was not how this was supposed to go. And now Ty is threatening to go to the cops? The cops? Give me a break. He doesn't have the balls.

I know I might have gone a little overboard, but it was almost as if the voice in my head just kept pushing me to do more. It was a rush. I couldn't stop myself. I knew how to get out of this mess—I was going to have to play the sympathy card. I was *not* going to jail. Fuck that. Worst case, I will use those pictures and videos to destroy them. I got collateral for a reason. I guess deep down, I knew I was going to have to cover my ass somehow.

Before it got any more out of hand, I decided to have a face-to-face chat with dear old dad and tell him my side of the story, and, hopefully, he would drop the whole idea of going to the cops. It's pretty much just my word against Marlon's.

When I got there, his whore for a nurse opened the door with her hand on her hip, looking me up and down with a stank attitude.

"Hello. Ty is straight to the back in the living room," she pointed.

"I know where it is. Thanks." Her energy was rude. I guess she heard the news too.

I took a deep breath as I saw Ty get up and walk toward me. He seemed larger than life when he was angry.

"Hi, Ty." I became a little nervous as I looked up at him sheepishly.

"No, 'Hi, Ty.' And save the puppy dog eyes, Journey. You want to tell me why you stole a check for five grand and then cashed it this morning on Peachtree Road at the check-cashing place?"

"Wait, noooo, no." I held my hand up. "Let's get this straight right now. I did *not* steal anything. Marlon wrote me that check as the donation for my lifestyle center fund. You know, that one I told you about?" Ty folded his arms and just stared at me. "He was very excited about it and wanted to help me. You can check with your bank. It's in his handwriting."

He waved me off. "Stop right there with the fucking lies. Marlon would never write a check for some big amount of money without running it by me. And I already ran a background check on you. I see you got forgery as one of your skills. Or was it because you drugged him to get him to do what you want? Your own mother told me about your little Devil's Breath prank."

"What? My mother is delusional. I don't use drugs. I didn't have to drug him. He wanted to get with me the second we met. Is this all about me sleeping with him because you know I'm grown, right? I can fuck who I want."

"Please cut the shit. You are going to jail, Journey. I don't give a fuck anymore. You're a damn psychopath."

"What? You take that back."

"Your whole attitude just shows how much you care about people. Unfortunately, your mom can't save you this time."

Papa started moaning in the background. Jocelyn was trying to console him. My hands began shaking because he was so loud, and it was starting to scare me.

"Jail? What are you talking about? My mother already paid you back, and I have loads of pictures and videos with Marlon, who was having a good time, and he does not look drugged. He was well aware of what he was doing, so I have proof that nothing went wrong."

"Yeah, about your proof. I heard it's pretty pornographic. Try to use any of that footage against him, and we will sue you for defamation."

"I wish you would try. But, who knows, it might just get leaked by a hacker." I shrugged my shoulders. He was not going to win.

Jocelyn screamed, "That's it, that's it. I can't let you do this anymore. What is *wrong* with you? Why are you so disrespectful? You wouldn't even be alive if it wasn't for this man. He's done nothing but be kind to you, and *this* is how you repay him? Being a damn thief?"

I turned to her and said, "I'm so sorry, but this is none of your business."

"Who do you think you're talking to, little girl?" Jocelyn ran up to me and got up in my face.

I calmly responded while I looked her up and down. "I'm not a little girl, and you need to back the fuck up before I show you."

Ty's voice was low and stern. "That's it, Journey. I need you to go now, or I'm calling the cops. Get out."

"Oh no, I'm not done. I want to make sure you know that I did not steal anything. Marlon was very generous. Now, you made my mother pay you back, so we have nothing else to fight over."

"You're crazy. He said to get out," Jocelyn screamed. "I'll help you out." She grabbed my arm. I pulled away and punched her in the face. She grabbed my hair and pulled it into a knot. I had so much adrenaline rushing through me that I didn't feel any pain. I bowed my head and charged into her stomach to get her on the floor, then fell on top of her. We wrestled, and then I felt Ty's hands pulling us apart.

He yelled, "Journey, stop it. Stop it."

I tried to get in a few punches, and Jocelyn kicked me when he pulled us apart.

"Get out of my house. I'm done. I'm done with youuuu! Get the fuck out!"

Papa was yelling and crying in the background.

I tried to hold it in, but I just fell apart and started crying. I pointed at Jocelyn. "You fucking bitch. This is *my* family. *My* family. *Not* yours."

I shouted into Jocelyn's mind, *You just lie there. Don't move a muscle until I say so. Just mind your own fucking business. You need to lie there and don't move until I leave.*

Jocelyn screamed, "Get her out of here before I kill her." She moved her head and was trying to get up. "I-I can't move. I can't moooove. I can't feel my legs. Ty, help!"

Ty ran over to her and got on his knees. He tried to lift her, but Jocelyn lay there paralyzed. I just smiled. I knew it would be over when I left, but they didn't. He looked up at me as I fixed my hair to the way it was and adjusted my clothes after that fight.

"What did you do? What did you doooo?"

Papa started crying and looked at me so coldly. He usually never made eye contact, but he looked right through me and shouted, "Ooooh, Diablaaaa."

Jocelyn moaned. "I think I just sprained something in my back when she fell on me. I don't know what's going on. My legs and arms won't move."

She was like a stiff board. I had no idea I could do that too. My powers must increase when I'm angry. That bitch got me so mad.

Ty got up and rushed me. He grabbed my shoulders and shook me. "What did you do to her? Did you give her that drug?"

I spit at him, and he slapped my face so hard.

"Are you out of your fucking mind? You spit on me?" He wiped his face in disgust. He was so tall and overpowering, and I was terrified. He looked like he had lost all self-control. My first reflex was to grab something near me. I thought he was going to hit me again. I yelled, *Stop, stop it* in his mind, but it didn't work.

He started to push me to the door. I barely felt my feet touch the ground, the way he picked me up. I tried to hold on to a wall. "Get out of my house now."

I grabbed a glass award in a teardrop shape off the bookshelf.

"Put that down. Put it down. Stop now. I don't want to hurt you."

"You already did. You slapped meeee," I screamed. "You *hit* meeee."

He reached in his pocket for his cell and called 911. "Yes, there's been an altercation and theft I'd like to report." He turned around to check on Jocelyn. I charged at him with the award. I hit him as hard as I could in the back of his head. He grabbed his head, then fell to the ground.

I heard a lot of voices in my head saying, *Fire, fire . . . Leave now. Jump. Jump.*

I felt dizzy and overwhelmed. Why did this have to go so wrong? Why couldn't he just be my dad? Just be there for me? Not lie to me. Why did he have to get so close with Natalia? He never really wanted me.

***

I suddenly smelled smoke and looked at Jocelyn on the floor. Then I looked at Papa, but I thought the smoke was coming from the kitchen. Ty was not moving, and he was a little farther away from Jocelyn. Both of them were on the ground, and Papa saw it all. It's a good thing he couldn't talk much because I was going to leave. I didn't want to burn up and die with the rest of them. I saw flames closing in on me, and I was terrified. *Jump, jump, or you will burn.*

My spirit guides were saving me. They were warning me to escape.

Jocelyn screamed, "You fucking bitch. What did you do to him? Help, somebody, help us!" she cried.

I looked at Papa, and he cried and pointed at me, "Diabla. You are the devil."

Ty started to bleed out on the marble floor from his head, and a part of me wanted to save him, but instead, I'd save myself. If anything, I would say he attacked me. I was *not* going to jail, and I was not going to burn up in here with them.

And so I jumped.

Chapter 21

Ty

My face pressed against the hard, cold marble floor. My head was heavy and pounding with a migraine. My mouth had the metallic taste of blood in it. The muscles in my body were so stiff. My memory was foggy. I didn't know where I was or what time it was. How long had I been lying here? However long it's been, I was slowly awakening from the autumn chill wrapping around my body.

A window was open, and I took a deep breath of the air it offered. I was glad to be alive. I didn't remember what had happened. I knew in my gut that whatever took place earlier could have killed me. Goose bumps formed on my arms.

Screams of terror from outside shook me to my core, but I could barely move. They were so loud. Somehow, I knew I was lucky. I felt as if my life were going to change forever. It was then I realized I was in my living room. I heard a slow drag of feet coming toward me. It was all coming together now.

I was disoriented but awakened by the screams from the crowd outside. My mouth was full of blood, and I felt a lump on the back of my head. I slowly touched it, and it was wet from my blood. Papa's feet were slowly drawing toward me. I heard Jocelyn screaming on the other side of the couch.

Papa was smiling at me, looking down at me on the ground. Then, without moving his mouth, he told me, *She's gone. She jumped.*

She jumped? Dear God, she jumped. We heard the ambulance coming from my 911 call that went through. Jocelyn's paralysis seemed to go away miraculously after Journey jumped. She ran to look over the balcony to see.

"Oh my God." Jocelyn covered her mouth and looked back at me in horror.

Chapter 22

Papa

I never liked her. I knew the moment I saw her she was one of us, but I also knew she was trouble. Her soul was not pure. She held a lot of resentment and always wanted to win.

I may not be able to speak like I used to, but I see and hear everything. I'm alive in here. I'm inside this rotting shell of a body, but my mind works just fine. I knew it from the start. She was a bad seed. Every bloodline has one or two.

Journey knew how to get what she wanted. She knew how to manipulate you, my grandson, who wants nothing but the best for everyone. But unfortunately for her, she did not count on this little invalid man to be even more powerful than the two of you combined.

When you lose some functions in your body, other ones will overcompensate. That is what happened to me. My gifts increased tremendously, and I had no one to tell. I told you not to open the door, Ty, but no one listens to me. I wanted you to hear me, but you were so wound up with anger you didn't take a moment. You thought I was just mumbling foolishness or remembering something from a TV show. But it was much more than that. I saw visions of what was to come. I was gifted at reading people all my life. I have had premonitions since I was a child. I knew Journey was a troubled soul from the start. I saw how stressed you were getting from her, Tylercito, and today was the last straw.

First, she hit my sweetheart Jocelyn and then tried to make her paralyzed. I could not believe my eyes, and it hurt me so much that I couldn't move fast enough to stop her. After that, I lost all compassion for her with whatever demon she struggled with, and I just wanted her to go away.

Jump, jump. There is a fire—jump. You will burn. I was able to wake Jocelyn up after Journey hit you in the head.

Call the cops . . . Tell them to come now. Call the cops, I said in her mind.

Jocelyn looked at me with love in her eyes because she knew it was me and couldn't believe it. She crawled over to you, Ty, to see if you were okay. Then she got up slowly. I don't know how many times I spoke to her, and she finally heard me. Jocelyn would tell you all the time that I knew what was going on between you, and she was right. I knew everything.

When she called the cops, I walked over slowly to check on you, grandson, and I saw that you were breathing with a bit of blood by your head and mouth from falling on your face. You just had a bruise and maybe will need some stitches, but you will be fine. I was furious. She was so evil. You looked around like you couldn't tell where you were, and then you saw my slippers coming toward you. After Journey jumped, all we heard was yelling from people outside.

"She jumped!"

"Oh my God."

"Call an ambulance!"

"A girl jumped. Must be suicide."

"Is she alive?"

I wiped the blood dripping from my nose. Today, I worked more than I ever had to. The best part is that *no one except you two* will ever know it was the little old man with the cane who did it.

I looked over the balcony to see the ambulance take Journey's body away. Everyone down there was worried, and I'm so sorry innocent people had to see that, but all I could do now was take a big sigh of relief.

Epilogue

Ty

So, that is how I ended up here—on the floor, kissing marble. My abuelo, Pedro Garcia, a.k.a. Papa, was the hero. Just goes to show the old man had more guts than I did.

La Diabla was definitely what she turned into. That's what she was. Unfortunately, my living nightmare, Daddy's little girl, was not who she claimed to be.

Everyone was free now. Our journey to hell was finally over.

The End

About the Author

Simone Kelly is an author, filmmaker, and the CEO of Own Your Power® Communications, Inc., where she assists many as a Holistic Business and Intuitive Life Coach. Originally from the Bronx, New York, Simone currently resides in Atlanta, Georgia.